Falling into a Summer Sky
Anthology

Anchorette Rousseau
C.J. Wood
Carrie Humphrey
K.R. Cervantez
Melinda Reynolds

Table of Contents

Lord of the Wood
Anchorette Roussseau
With the crush of people and dealing with being the executor of her grandfather's estate, the dark, cool woods call to Lucille on this hot, summer day. What memories, fears, or delights await her there?

A Georgia Summer
C.J. Wood
When Collie heads down to Georgia, she expects a relaxing, albeit boring, summer helping out her MawMaw. What she doesn't expect is a brewing romance with the ridiculously attractive farm hand, making the summer anything but boring.

A Summer Solstice Mistake
Carrie Humphrey
Summer days are long, the nights short, and both bring out Demons of all kinds. Nastia is used to hunting them, and being hunted in return, but in one fleeting moment, one hot and heavy decision, she gets more than she bargained for.

Summer Wings
K.R. Cervantez

When Drake greets his new partner, she is not at all what he expected and he discovers that he likes it. As Kallima and Drake investigate the recent mermaid murders, they learn more about each other and the mutual attraction they share.

The Root of the Apocalypse: Part 1
Becoming Rose
Melinda Reynolds

Summertime......a time for friends, merriment and folly. In the heart of a contagion, can two friends find time for either?

Dedication

We would like to dedicate this book, and these stories, to everyone who have continuously supported us through our writing, our lives, and our adventures.

To friends and family who thought we might be a tad crazy, but went along with us anyway, thank you.

To the authors that inspire us. Thank you for your words, your worlds, and your imagination so that we may dive into our own and not be afraid to share what we have discovered.

Lord of the Wood
Anchorette Rousseau

Summer is one of those times where you can be alone or be surrounded by people at a moment's notice, depending on your whim at the time. It is a sort of liminal time and place, where the heat and alcohol numb our senses, and unlike the numb of deep winter, the heat allows us to go outside and explore, the lush fecundity of nature is at its highest and our raw, natural selves know it, even though the veneer of civility tries to fool us into thinking otherwise.

Outside, with a glass of rum and cola, the ice in the plastic cup causing condensation to run down the side, just as the heat from the summer sweat does my back, I stand in the forest at the edge of my grandfather's property and listen. I can't take the mournful revelers any longer, they are playing at being sad while filling their bellies with food at the expense of the old man's passing. "Tradition," they will say, and they aren't wrong. In the American South, when someone dies, everyone brings over food, enough food to last for weeks, and we eat until we are stuffed and cannot eat another bite, talk about the 'good old days' with our beloved dead, cry at memories, and then drive home to sleep off the food haze we've put ourselves in, to go back to our normal lives the next day. Only the deceased is no longer with us, and their fridge is filled to bursting with our leftovers and someone has to deal with all of their paperwork and household belongings and all that food and left over medicine. I don't want to hear the laughing or the crying. I don't want to hear any of it. I want the quiet, which has been lacking for weeks now, as rounds of visitors have come and gone from the house in saying their goodbyes. People who haven't come in twenty or thirty years arrived up the long driveway in the past weeks, and have arrived again today, only to be gone tonight, never to return.

"Go take a breather," the minister said, putting his bony arm on my shoulder. "I don't think any will blame you if you take a little time for yourself." So I took myself out side, first to the deck, then to the backyard, but still people linger.

The woods beacon me, the lowering temperature of the sweltering heat of the summer has arms that reach out for me in the shape of branches and dark cool moss. I take another swig of my rum and cola and sigh. My feet are following an old path, one that my brothers and cousins took as a child, played on and found so many secret and wonderful places. Have other children been on this path in their wanderings? I don't know. Electronics, phones and video games tend to keep them indoors nowadays. Do they explore wild places like we did when we were younger? Do they know the secret things that the woods hold, the fears and wonders that even as an adult still call to me and repel me as my feet walk the familiar pathway all these years later? I hear the leaves rustle, the chattering of birds and squirrels, sounds I recognize and sounds I don't know coming at me from the forest as I walk.

Taking another sip from my drink, I breath in

8

deep of the air, wet and hot, the breath of the place, smelling of living and dying things here in the forest, Spanish moss dripping from the branches like water, all suffering from the summer like the rest of us.

I was the most surprised of everyone when the old man asked me to come and help take care of him. We'd parted ways when I was a teenager, under unkind words, and I hadn't been back.

"You have decide if you want to go," my husband had told me. He'd never met the old man, or any of the family close to him. We hadn't invited him to our wedding or children's christenings or any other important occasion. It was as if they were dead to us and us to them. "But if you don't go, and you regret it, you won't get the chance back."

It was those last words that made me chose to go see what the old man wanted. My husband was rarely that wise, so the fact that he gave such sage advice that this time was worth listening to. I wasn't expecting an apology, and of course, I sure as hell wasn't going to give one. And I could always just get in my car and leave whenever I wanted to. I was an adult, under no obligation to stay in this old fashioned southern wannabe estate with a bunch of old fashioned southern fuddy duddies that never got the memo that the antebellum period ended about 150 years ago.

When I drove up the drive that first day, the feeling of familiarity that enveloped me was horrifyingly comfortable. I loved it and hated it at the same time. The house hadn't changed at all, it was like going back in time to my childhood, which back then had been like going back in time to who knew when, with fine china in hutches along walls, oriental carpets donning the floor and hound dogs running around the property baying at unlikely things. There were no hound dogs this time around, the old man must have given up hunting a long time ago, or dog breeding, or both. Or perhaps the woods had taken the dogs and kept them, as punishment for something the old man had done, or something one of us had done, and poor little things had to pay the price for it.

"Lucille," the old man said when he saw me. He was a pitiful sight. He had to stay in the living room all the time now, he had no mobility. The hospice bed was where the antique chaise used to be, and where one of the hutches filled with old china used to reside, now a monitor and IV stand with a morphine drip lived. Both his lawyer, a minister, and a hospice nurse were with him when I arrived. "You didn't bring your family?"

I shook my head. "No, sir. I didn't know what I would be bringing them into," I replied honestly.

He nodded and the minister laughed. "He said you and he were a lot alike."

The old man pointed at me and smiled, toothless. It didn't appear they were letting him wear his false teeth any longer. "She was always the most honest."

Ah, so that was why he chose the prodigal granddaughter.

The lawyer began to regale me about how I was to be in charge of the old man's affairs, the executor of his estate when he died, etc, etc, until I held up a hand. He continued to talk, so I had to cut him off with a sharp sound like used with my children when they were toddlers.

"If I choose to," I told him.

"Excuse me?" the lawyer asked.

"I will do this if I choose to," I told him.

I fully expected the old man to jump out of his bed and start beating me the with the tube of his morphine IV, but apparently he was beyond that at this point.

The lawyer, who apparently hadn't anticipated that I would know enough about the law to know I would have a choice in the matter straightened up, frowning. "Do you choose to, Miss Lucille?" he drawled.

I hated that drawl.

There was a moment of silence before I glanced at the nurse. "Aren't you going to weight in?" I asked.

"My job is make sure he is comfortable," she stroked the old man's arm.

I sighed. "I'll do it."

"Are you comfortable sir?" she asked the old man.

He chuckled. "More comfortable than I've been in a long time," he said.

He died seven weeks after that day.

And now everyone's in the house saying how sad it is that he's gone, when he was a bastard that lived as long as he did out of spite. He made me executor out of spite. Do you know how hard it is to be executor of a place like this to a family like this? They're all bastards, they're all spiteful, and they all want what doesn't belong to them. I have a full mind to give the entire thing to charity and be done with it.

I've come deep enough into the forest now that the noise from the house is gone, and the only sounds are the living, breathing forest itself. It occurs me to then, suddenly, as if the thought is not mine, that perhaps the old man did not call for me to be his executor. That perhaps the forest did, as it is calling to me now. I sit down on an old stump, placing my almost empty cup on a flat rock and listen around me, as I used to when I was young and forced to come here. The forest was a refuge, a place to get away from the rules and regulations of the house and the old man. Sometimes her cousins were afraid of it, and sometimes she was too, but she was still brave enough to venture in it.

In her very early teens, before she'd left for good, a large group of them had been tramping about, looking for a watering hole that occasionally popped up during the wet season. Laden with fishing gear, they started to explore, only to be turned about by the living woods several times, followed by strange noises and even freaked out by the feeling of being watched and the whispers of voices just outside of their hearing. She had been the one to follow the whispers, to disprove them as real, even though she heard them as well. In her mind, she thought, *Either they are a person playing pranks or a they are ghost. If they are a ghost, then they don't have a body and they can't hurt us. If they are a person playing a prank, we can jump on them and beat them up.* It hadn't occurred to her that her cousins would run and leave her at the hands of a perhaps ax murderer had the whispers been coming from one of them.

She had thought she'd seen movement in the woods, green against green, brown against brown, as if the woods itself was caressing its own body like a scarf does in the wind. Perhaps it was a trick of her eyes, or a trick of the light, or a trick of the movement of the leaves in the shadows of the dappled darkness in the summer heat. She followed it, along with the whispers, to find herself in a small open space in the forest she had never seen before.

Looking behind her, she saw that none of her cousins had followed her, leaving her alone and feeling very lost in the now quiet space. In front of her, the movement happened again, sienna caressing green brown, and out of the colors of the forest, a being appeared. It looked like a walking tree, its body made of bark, except that its face was sideways. The mouth, shaped like that of a human being, was wide with many teeth and hung open, but it hung open from side to side, not up and down. It had no nose that I could see, and instead of two eyes, it had several dotted about what looked like the top of its head. "One of a thousand of young," the whispers, which before had been unintelligible, were now clear to my ears.

"I am one of a thousand young," I had answered, being the only thing I could think to say. It was unreal, like a dream, or a nightmare, that I thought it had to be one, the way the sunshine was glinting off of the creature, making the greens more green and the browns more brown.

I think it might have nodded, I am not sure, but it blinked many of its eyes, none of them in unison. I heard a snap behind me, glanced around very quickly, to make sure it wasn't another of the creatures. When I saw nothing, I turned back, but the creature was gone, having blended back into the woods from which it had emerged.

I'd stomped loudly back to my cousins, who hadn't moved from where they'd stopped, and scolded them all soundly. I told them I hadn't found the source of the words, I'd gained the reputation of being brave, level headed, and a little bit brash. It had proven to myself that I was fully aware I could function while scaring myself out of my wits.

Kind of like right now.

The hair on the back of my neck and my arms is rising, and I can feel the forest watching. That creature that I saw in that daydream all those years ago, I was sure that I hadn't imagined it. It was as real as if it had been standing in front of me, as real as the old man who had called me back to this cursed place because was the most honest of his progeny. What did honesty have to do with anything? Maybe he wanted me to give all of this away to charity.

Like that day all those years ago, the woods seemed to move on themselves, like rubbing its hands together to create even more heat in the humid summer. The Spanish moss moved, even though there was no breeze in the trees, and the strange silence of the forest pressed on me.

"One of a thousand young," I sigh, the memory of long ago forefront in my mind. This day is much like that one, dank and restless, the feeling of something about to burst through, just on the other side of my vision or hearing, but I am unable to reach it.

"You are one of a thousand young," says a soft voice, much like a hiss from the forest. "But you are only one who is here."

I do not turn my face to the noise, because I am afraid. I admit it. My heart beats fast in my chest, threatening to constrict my throat. I keep my eyes straight ahead, swallowing the humid air in an attempt to find words. "There are plenty of people at the house," I reply.

"I don't want any of the people at the house," replies the forest. I hear the suss of the movement, again the Spanish moss waves in the breeze-less air. The voice caresses the bark like a water does the rocky ground of the creek, moving to match the shape of the thing it is beside with no effort. "You are who I have always wanted. You, brave one, who are one of a thousand young."

I turn, then, to face the thing that is speaking, because the movement is pressing on my body, even though nothing is touching me. It is as if I can feel it, but it is a good twenty feet from me, difficult to distinguish between the trees and branches, the dappled sunlight and the moss hanging from the wood. It makes no sound, but seems to absorb it, to eat it, deciding what sounds of forest to allow to emanate and which to suck into itself.

It takes all my willpower not to run. Standing there among the trees is a tall animal, but it isn't an animal, but a man. Only, it isn't a man, but a demon. But it isn't a demon, it is a thing that has no name, that could try to be described but wouldn't be able to. It is at least seven feet tall, the fur that covers its body is the color of moss covered tree bark, black and brown and green. It's chest, wide and muscled, reminds me of a man that lifts things for a living, like a lumber jack or a construction worker, arms that work to move items from location to another, weight being no object, they would be beautiful, except that they belong to the head of a goat.

The black horns roll in circles on the side of its head, huge, like tree branches emerging from a black trunk. The ears, long and slender, rested underneath them, framing the goat face, where two large, golden hourglass goat eyes look at me with a soft glow in the low light of the forest. Along its neck and muscled shoulders, matching goat eyes, all with hourglass pupils, dot its form, blinking out of sync with each other as it regards me.

"I am no one," I whisper, unable to move. When you read in a book that someone is froze with fear, that is not an exaggeration. They are, their body will not work. You tell your legs to run, your arms to flail, your lungs to inhale, and none of your body will follow your commands. You are simply still, in hopes that by doing so the danger will pass and you will be able to run for you life when it does. Until then, you are trapped as sure as if you were under a spell of some sort.

"My mother is pleased with you," it says, moving toward me. The movement makes it clear it is a he, the phallus the pats against its hairy thigh leaves no doubt of that. My eyes continue down to its feet, which are the hooves of a goat, cloven, but make no sound as it walks

15

on the forest floor toward me. "You, brave one, who is one of her thousands of young."

"I am?" I ask quickly, managing to stand up, but I can make myself move no further.

He seems undisturbed by my standing. "Few are they who can look upon the Lord of the Wood and tell the tale afterward," he says, all of his golden eyes blinking softly. They are disconcerting, how they do not blink in unison, but at different rates, scattered as they are over his head and shoulders, like dapples of sunlight through the trees.

I swallow hard, for though I am afraid, I am also intrigued. Just as I was all those year ago when I almost saw him. But I didn't see him then, only his movements among the forest. Now, he is in the light, away from the branches, for me to see in his full glory. I am afraid, I cannot deny that. But understanding starts to flicker in my mind. "You called me here," I say.

"I call many here," he answers.

I do not like how non-committal his reply is. "Will the funeral goers all come running?" I ask. I notice there is a bit of mania in my voice, and I am not sure if it is the fear or the rum that is giving it to me.

He shakes his head, again his many eyes blinking out of unison, and takes a step toward me. It is tentative, as if he is afraid I will run away. And perhaps I will, because my legs are telling me to do so, that this is dangerous, that I shouldn't stay here, in this clearing, with this monster, this Lord of the Wood. But I do, anyway, because I am not sure my legs would obey me if I told them to run.

"They are not the brave ones," he answers. "You are the one who has always been the most honest, the most brave."

"What does that have to do with anything?" I ask.

16

He takes another step toward me, his hooves making no sound. I want to run, but at the same time, I want him near, I want to reach out to touch him, in his beautiful grotesqueness, to feel the heart of the forest beneath my fingers, that has chosen to show itself to me.

"The bravery allows you to see," he says, taking another step closer. He reaches his hand out, the hand of a man, and it hovers near my cheek, as all of his eyes, scattered on his goat face and neck look at me. "The honesty allows you to know."

I furrow my brow. The fear inside of me is the base of all of my other feelings now, my confusion a part of it. "To know what?"

His hand slips behind my neck, gentle as that of a lover, and he says, "Me."

Suddenly his fingers grasp my skin, and he pulls me toward him. His goat mouth is open, I can see his large, flat teeth, his many eyes looking at me, and I almost wet myself, letting out a squeak of fear. I close my eyes, waiting for the pain to come, to be eaten alive by this monster, to be impaled by a horn, to be stomped by hooves. But instead, soft lips press to mine, strong arms wrap themselves around me, crush me against the body of the Lord of the Wood, my breath, gone from fear, now stolen from surprise.

For a moment, the world is still. I can feel the softness of his lips as he parts my mouth, his tongue, that of a man, inside my mouth. I can feel the hair on his chest against my collarbone, under my fingers as I rest my hands on his shoulders, I feel the lashes of one his eyes blink against my palm. The heat of the summer has invaded my body, but his body seems to be a different temperature altogether, the coolness of the earth, the dampness of the moss. No sounds reach my ears, even my heartbeat in my own head is silenced for a moment

17

and there is him.

I realize I want him. I want him like I have wanted nothing in my life. I do not know what I am supposed to do, for it seems that he, too, is frozen in this kiss, his hand hasn't moved, only his lips on mine, his tongue in my mouth, the rest of him is a cool statue against me, save the blinking eye under my palm. It is as if he is waiting for me, but waiting for what?

I take a step into him, wrap my arms around him, press my lips to him, my body to him, open my mouth and hear the silence of the woods around me. Opening my eyes, I can see all of his golden orbs glowing in the low light, their hourglass pupils looking at me, blinking out of sync, almost hypnotically. The pressure of the proof of his maleness is pressing against my thigh, only the thin fabric of my black summer dress separating us.

I am breathing heavily, and the moisture between my legs is not just from the heat and humidity of the forest. I know it him, the musk from his body, the silence of the forest, the strength of his arms around me. I lost it once, long ago, and I am determined not to lose the chance again. It may be a mad delirium brought on by the stress of acting as executor of the old man's estate, of memories of the past, of the dance of dueling relatives and a complicated will. I am going to engage in another dance at the moment.

I slide my hands up his head, so I grasp both of his horns, not sure what I am doing or what purpose it will serve once I have done it, but it seems to be what he was looking for. He sinks down to his knees, bringing me with him, his weight more than I expect, and lays me down on the moss of the clearing. The only sound is he and I and the silence of the forest.

Then, I am alone, with the moving of the leaves around me, the forest caressing itself, the smell of the earth filling my nostrils. The stump that I used as a seat is next to me, my empty glass is on it. I stand up, smoothing my black sundress, plucking the dried leaves out of my hair, picking up my empty glass.

Goosebumps rise on my skin as a breeze wends its way through the shrubbery. I tilt my head and listen, but the silence of the woods is gone. The crickets sing, frogs croak, and in the distance I can hear the gathered crowds of the old man's funeral. Perhaps, on another day, I will come back here and wander the forest, listening to the whispers that were just out of my hearing. Maybe that time, I will be able to understand what they say.

A Georgia Summer
C.J. Wood

What am I doing? Collie thought to herself for what seemed to be the millionth time that day. She was ten hours into her drive from New York City to Georgia, where she would be spending the entire summer with her MawMaw Lottie. Just thinking that sentence made her feel like a little girl on summer break from school, not a thirty year old woman with a career that she loved very, very much. But, when her Mom and Dad got a call from the hospital saying that MawMaw had fallen and broken her hip and consequently would need around the clock care, something had to be done. While her MawMaw did have a farm hand, Jerry, who lived onsight, Collie and her parents didn't want him to have to bear all the work of the farm plus the work of caring for Lottie. After a little bit of discussion, they decided it made the most sense for Collie to head down south, since her editing job could technically be done from anywhere as long as she had access to the internet. So here she was, on her way to a place that she considered to be hotter than hell. *God, I'm already sweating through my shirt.*

The drive was uneventful, and she eventually pulled into her MawMaw's farm. The sun was just starting to fall in the sky, much like Collie's eyelids were starting to droop down. After grabbing her bag from the trunk, she barely registered her surroundings as she stumbled into the front door. She was instantly on high alert when she walked into the living room. With her MawMaw still in the hospital, the house should have been silent. But was it? No. Collie could hear rummaging coming from the back of the house, causing her heart to stop beating for a couple of seconds. She quietly shut the door behind her, setting down her bag and grabbing her PawPaw's shotgun that was always resting next to the door. Her heart was kicking against her chest like a donkey, and she could feel her palms growing sweaty as she quietly walked back to the kitchen, expertly avoiding the floorboards that squeaked under the slightest amount of weight. When she peaked around the wall, she saw a muscular, but feminine, figure with short blonde hair standing rummaging through the pantry. Fully stepping around the wall, Collie cocked the gun.

"Who are you and what the fuck are you doing in my MawMaw's house?"

***

Jerry slowly put her hands up above her head in a "I mean no harm" motion. Lazily turning around, she came face to face with Lottie's granddaughter, Collie. Jerry had seen pictures of her, of course, Lottie had them placed all around the house, so she knew the girl was pretty. But seeing her in person? *Wow.* Her strawberry blonde hair was mused from the wind, and her blue eyes were alive with angry fire. And for the millionth time in her life, Jerry was glad she was a girl, because she was pretty sure if she was a guy? Yep, she'd definitely be sporting a hard-on.

"Are you going to answer me or am I going to have to shoot?"

"Now, I don't think Lottie would be very happy about her white cupboards being splattered with blood. Do you?" Jerry laughed as a confused look passed over Collie's face, and she decided to put the poor girl out of her misery by introducing herself. "Hi. I'm Jerry."

***

"You...you're Jerry?" Collie slowly lowered the point of the gun to the ground, but kept a tight grip on it, ready to use it if need be. Thinking back to the numerous times her MawMaw mentioned Jerry, she realized that there was never a mention of "him" or "he". Collie and her parents just assumed Jerry was a guy, and without thinking, Collie sputtered those words out. "I thought Jerry was a guy?"

"Oh, I am definitely a girl. Here, let me prove it to you." With a wink, "Jerry" started to raise her tank top, showing off the start of a very toned stomach.

"No-no-no. You don't need to do that!" Collie waved an arm frantically in front of her as she felt her inner temperature start to rise, causing her face to grow red in an embarrassing blush. "I believe you're a girl. It just caught me off guard. What are you doing in here anyways? Don't you live in the barn apartment?"

"I do. I just thought that it would be nice to bake Lottie a blackberry pie to welcome her home with." Jerry's southern drawl was well pronounced as she spoke, and it made something inside Collie flutter to life.

"Well, I guess since you know her favorite pie, you must be who you say you are," Collie said sarcastically. But as she rolled her eyes to the side, a certain picture on the fridge caught her attention. In the picture, the girl claiming to be Jerry was standing next to her MawMaw, who had an arm draped around Jerry's shoulder. *Ah hell, I guess she really is Jerry.*

***

Collie woke up the following morning after a pleasant evening cooking with Jerry. What wasn't so pleasant? The sound of knocking on her bedroom door at the ass crack of dawn.

"Go away!" Collie half yelled, half mumbled. She pressed her face into the pillow trying to block out the blinding sunlight.

"Get up. We have to get going." There was amusement in Jerry's voice, which further enraged Collie. She screamed into the pillow and kicked her feet up and down, throwing a full on temper tantrum. To say she wasn't a morning person would be an understatement.

"If you don't get up, I swear to god I will come in there and rip the sheets off of you like a child. Come on."

With one more groan, Collie sat up. As her eyes insisted on closing again, she heard the doorknob rattle as it slowly started to open. With an instant jolt of adrenaline, she scrambled off of the bed, holding the sheet tightly to her chest.

"Wait! I'm naked!" She expected for the door to instantly close, but instead it just stopped in its tracks. Neither opening more or closing. "Um… you going to close the door or…"

"Yeah, yeah...you always sleep naked?" Jerry's voice dripped with humor and a hint of flirtation.

"Not that it's any of your business. But, yes. It's more comfy that way….duh," Collie grumbled the words out as she grabbed up crumpled clothes from her bag. As the door closed silently, she could have sworn she heard Jerry say the words, "You could make it my business."

The smell of freshly brewed coffee welcomed Collie into the kitchen, and she quickly walked over and grabbed a coffee cup. As she was about to fill it up however, an arm came around from behind her and took away the cup, replacing it with a travel mug.

"No time. You know if we leave Lottie sitting in that hospital room for even a second longer than necessary she'll skin us alive." As Collie turned around to respond in affirmation, because she knew damn well MawMaw was not happy about being there, she brushed up against Jerry. Her breath caught in her lungs at the sudden heat that sufused her body, and her words were caught by a mysterious cat. She quickly stumbled back, and mumbled something about how she'd hurry up. After pouring way too much sugar into her coffee, which was just the way she liked it, she followed Jerry out to the truck. After she finished half her mug, she finally felt like she had the capacity to act somewhat like a human being.

"So is Jerry your actual name or is it short for something?" Jerry gave Collie a dubious look out of the side of her eye, but it was a couple minutes before she spoke.

"Geraldine." She mumbled out.

"Wait, what?" It took a second for Collie's brain to remind her of the question she initially asked. "Jerry stands for Geraldine?" There was a little bit of disbelief in Collie's voice as she spoke. *Talk about an old school name.*

"Really? This coming from a girl named *Collie*?"

"Heeey, It's a family name!" Collie shot back with a laugh, playfully slapping Jerry on the shoulder. Jerry smiled back and they lapsed into a surprisingly comfortable silence. Old school Johnny Cash played on the radio as green fields that were full of cattle flew by the window. Before she knew it, they were pulling into the small town hospital.

***

Jerry pulled into the parking lot feeling like her body was set ablaze. She had never been so affected by being in close quarters with another girl. Yeah, she had dated in the past, but this? This was an entirely different feeling. One that she had never felt before, especially considering that she just met Collie the night before. At least in person.

Jerry had started working for Lottie three years ago when her husband Abott was diagnosed with cancer. Ever since then Lottie constantly talked about her children, and even more so her wonderful granddaughter, Collie. Jerry had seen hundreds of pictures and home videos of Collie from when she was just a babe to when she graduated from NYU and started at Duke Publishing House. From the first moment Lottie started telling Jerry about Collie, she could tell the girl was special, and had always wanted to meet her. Everytime Collie and her parents came into town though, Jerry took the time off so she could visit her own family in Alabama. She never thought she'd actually have the chance to meet Collie. But here she was, in the passenger seat of her truck, strawberry colored hair tossed up into a messy bun.

As they got out and walked towards the building, Jerry put her hands in her jean pockets to keep herself from reaching out towards Collie. Once inside, they walked up to the receptionist for directions to Lottie's room, and after a couple of turns found the right place.

"Oh, I just cannot wait for you to meet her. She is just the best granddaughter an old bat like myself could ask for. Can you believe she is coming down here for the entire summer all the way from New York just to help out around the house? I told her I had Jerry, but she just wouldn't take no for an answer." Lottie's voice drifted through the door, causing a little groan of embarrassment to escape Collie's lips. As Jerry pushed through the partially opened door, she looked over to see Collie's face lit with joy.

"Mawmaw! How are you doing?" Collie asked as she bent down to give Lottie a hug, which was returned with more force than you'd think an old lady could muster. Jerry knew this from experience.

"I am ready to get out of here, my dear. Take me from this place right this instant. It is just an awful place to stay!" Jerry laughed as Collie quickly apologized to the nurse.

"Don't worry about it. My name is Birdie. I do home visits by the way, so if you ever need anything just give the hospital a ring and ask for me. I'm just going to go get a wheelchair and the paperwork, I'll be back in a shake and a jiffy." As the nurse walked out of the room, she looked over to see Collie checking Birdie out. *Well, guess that answers that question.*

"Now, Mawmaw, why didn't you tell us that Jerry was a girl?" Collie asked with some accusation in her voice. Lottie let out a bellowing laugh.

"Because what does it matter, my sweet girl?"

"It matters because when I walked in the house and saw a strange girl, I pulled a gun on her."

"Well now why would you pull a gun on my Jerry-girl?"

"Because MawMaw. I was tired, I heard someone in the kitchen, and then there was a girl standing there. Like I said, we all assumed Jerry was a guy. I panicked." As Collie started to laugh, Lottie joined in and reached over to pull Jerry into a hug.

"Well, I am so sorry Jerry," Lottie said with humor still dripping in her voice.

"Don't worry about it, Lottie. Besides, I told her you'd have a connipshit if she shot me and got blood all over your kitchen."

"Darn tootin'!" Lottie nodded vigorously, as laughter filled the room again. After some more catching up between Collie and Lottie, Birdie was back in the room and they were soon heading back to the homestead.

*　*　*

When they pulled back up the long driveway to her MawMaw's house, Collie was finally awake enough to take in her surroundings. The white house was built in the traditional plantation style, columns included, and was surrounded by fifty acres of green pastures.

As they drove up the winding driveway, Collie looked out the window to see the many Saanen goats, which were grouped into different pastures. They were, in her humble opinion, the best breed of goats around. She smiled brightly at all the memories of her playing with them as she grew up. As they parked the truck however, Collie noticed three different pastures with a much smaller breed of goat.

"Oh my god—"

"Do not use the Lord's name in vain young—"

"Yeah, sorry MawMaw, but more importantly, when did you get Pygmy Goats!?!?" Collie let out a little squeal of excitement. While she considered Saanens to be the best, you could *not* beat tiny goats. Her MawMaw let out a little laugh, but it was Jerry who responded.

"Nigerian Dwarf Goats. And we started the herd back in January. A couple of does are actually due to give birth in the next few weeks." An excited squeal from Collie was her only response.

After getting her MawMaw settled in her favorite chair, Jerry went back out to do her daily work, and Collie was left alone. Figuring she should also get to work, she pulled out her laptop. Collie hadn't realized how accustomed to the sounds of New York she had grown over her life. Here she sat in the quiet of farm life, devoid of honking cars, sirens blaring by, and people shouting on the streets, and she could not stay focused on the book she was trying to edit. Okay, okay, maybe it wasn't so much the lack of noises, but the addition of an extremely attractive woman she frequently saw outside the window. With her shoulder length blonde hair, and a welcoming smile, Jerry was definitely a distraction. Collie got up and closed the blinds. *Ah, much better. No distractions for me!* After another couple hours of work though, she decided a break was deserved.

Going outside, she found Jerry in one of the far paddocks playing with some of the does and their kids.

"Working hard or hardly working?" Collie shouted out as she approached. She did her best to mimic her PawPaw's voice, who frequently asked her the same thing when she came to visit.

"Oh, definitely working hard. Someone has to tame these wild beasts." As soon as she spoke, one of the kids tried to jump up on her back, and quickly fell off, causing a cute little giggle to escape Jerry's throat. "I do need to go and milk the does up at the main barn though, want to lend me a hand?"

"That's why I came down here."

As Jerry drove them up to the barn in the 4-wheeler, Collie finally asked Jerry something that had been bothering her.

"So, if you've worked here for a couple of years now, how is it that this is our first time meeting?"

"Ah, my family actually lives in Alabama. So whenever you and your parents came, I took the time to go visit them."

"That makes sense. Well, I'm glad we were finally able to meet." Collie gave a shy smile, which was thankfully returned by a much brighter smile from Jerry as she agreed to the statement. They spent the rest of the afternoon milking goats, joking around and talking about this and that. And flirting. There was definitely some flirting going on, and it was with a much brighter smile that Collie started to walk back to the house to make sure her MawMaw was still doing okay. Before she walked out the doors, Jerry called out to her.

"Thanks for the help, Las."

"Las? I'm Irish, not Scottish," Collie called back.

"No, it's short for Lassie." Jerry winked as Collie just smiled and shook her head. It's not the first time anyone had tried calling her Lassie. However it was the first time someone used it as a pet name and not an insult. *I think I could actually like that nickname coming from her.*

***

After a couple of weeks flew by, Jerry and Collie had fallen into an unspoken routine. Jerry would do her usual work in the morning while Collie got her own work done and took Lottie to her physical therapy sessions. When Collie returned in the afternoon she would join Jerry in the main barn for the afternoon milking. And while they did get the milking done, they spent a lot more time shamelessly flirting by way of seeing who could out cheese each other by cliche pick up lines. And some play wrestling. Apparently learning self defence was a necessity for any girl living in the big, bad city, and while Jerry thought of herself as being pretty capable, Collie knew some seriously cool moves.

Today was no different, other than the fact that the sunny Georgia sky had quickly turned dark about an hour before hand, and the heavy rains that followed had yet to let up. As Jerry waited for Collie to show up, she found herself eagerly pacing, a giddiness that was becoming her new best friend filling her stomach. *Stop it Jerry, she is returning home when the summer ends and you will just be left here with a broken heart!* Despite the wonderful pep talk, one that she gave herself basically everyday, she still found herself falling for the fun and sarcastic Collie. Cheesy lines such as "You can't help who you love," and "The heart wants what the heart wants" flew through her mind, counteracting her daily inner monologue where she called herself an idiot. Glancing at her phone, she realized that she had been absently pacing for a good fifteen minutes. A feeling of unease chased away the butterflies in her stomach, and she quickly walked over to the house to see that Collie and Lottie had yet to return. *It's probably fine. It's raining super hard and Collie is a safe driver. She's probably just driving much slower than usual. That's why she's late.* Jerry tried to reason with herself as she sat on the porch, watching the driveway and waiting for Collie's car to come creeping into sight. When four o'clock hit, she had turned into a ball of anxiety. Collie was officially an hour late. With the roads leading up to Lottie's farm being dirt, not highly trafficked, and the reception out here being piss poor at best, Jerry wasn't sure that Collie would actually be able to reach out to anyone for help if she needed it.

With sudden determination, Jerry ran to grab her keys and jumped into her truck. She went barrelling down the driveway before reminding herself that if she got into a crash she would be of little use. With her teeth gritted, she slowed down to a much more reasonable speed, her grip growing tighter around the steering wheel with each passing second. She drove slowly down the country highway, hazards on, while frantically looking to either side of the road. After only a couple of miles, she rounded a bend and her heart stopped in her chest for a second before starting in triple time. On the side of the road walking her way was Collie. She was absolutely drenched, her thin shirt and shorts sticking to her pale skin, skin that seemed to be much paler than usual.

Leaping out of the truck, utter relief rushed through her. *She's okay, she's really okay.* With her mind solely on those thoughts, she ran up to Collie and without thinking embraced her in a tight hug, smashing her lips into Collie's.

***

Despite the sudden afternoon showers, the day had started like any other. Hot as hell and sunny as heaven. As far as Collie knew, it was going to end like any other, with her helping Jerry in the barn and shamelessly flirting. Collie was lying to herself and her MawMaw when she said the flirting was just innocent fun, however. Because yes, she had just finished having the most embarrassing conversation with her MawMaw who had outright asked her if milking goats was "all her and Jerry were up to."

"It's nothing, MawMaw. We get along well and are comfortable around each other, but that's all it is. Besides, Jerry doesn't like me like that… and besides that, I'm heading home at the end of the summer. I'm not some naive girl who thinks some grand summer romance is going to happen."

"Do not lie to me young lady, I see the way you two look at each other. It reminds me of when Abott first started courting me." Collie looked out of the corner of her eye to see a far off look cross over her MawMaw's face, a sad smile playing at her lips. The fact that her MawMaw could see right through her was not surprising. She had known Collie was gay almost before Collie knew, and was the one who helped her come out to both herself and her parents.

Collie returned her attention to her driving, trying her best to navigate the dirt road through the downpour that was assaulting this particular section of Georgia. She was going much slower than usual, but with distracting thoughts of Jerry running through her mind, it was straight up dangerous on the roads. Without warning, the car started fishtailing, and try as she might, Collie could not get the car under control. An eerie calm fell over her as the car went into the ditch.

"MawMaw, are you okay!?" Collie asked once the car finally stopped. Her MawMaw swatted away the arm that Collie had thrown in front of her chest in a protective gesture.

"I was already in pain from that darned PT session, this felt like a cakewalk. I am fine my dear." Collie was unaware that she was holding her breath until her MawMaw finished talking, and she quickly released it.

"Okay good. Let me get out my phone and... oh great, no service. Shall we just wait here for someone to show up then?" Although the ditch wasn't that deep, they would still need to be towed out of it in order to get safely back on the road.

"Oh yes, let's just sit here for hours in the rare case that someone may drive by and isn't an axe murderer. No, my dear, I think you should start walking home."

"Walk home?! But what if that axe murderer pulls over and murders me, MawMaw? Murders me with an axe!? Because he's an axe murderer?!" Sarcasm laced Collie's voice as she jokingly responded to her MawMaw. It wasn't the first time she had mentioned axe murderers, and it had quickly become an inside joke between her and Jerry.

After her MawMaw just stared back at her, she finally acquiesced and got out into the pouring rain. She was quickly soaked to the bone, and a chill had started over her entire body. She was officially angry with her MawMaw and couldn't quite figure out the flawed logic in her MawMaw's argument. *Surely Jerry will come find us eventually? Come on Jerry!*

After what felt like hours, she saw Jerry's truck slowly approaching. *Hallelujah!* Collie almost screamed it out loud, hands up to the sky, but that would have taken way too much energy. So instead she just imagined it. A large smile spread on her face when Jerry pulled over and started running toward her. As soon as they were in arms length of each other, Jerry pulled her into a tight hug. As Collie turned her head up to say thank you, Jerry's lips crashed down onto hers. As Jerry's tongue flicked out to run across the seam of Collie's closed lips, she eagerly opened up with a gasp. Their tongues met in a synchronized dance, like they had done this countless times before. This wasn't Collie's first kiss by any means, but was it her best? Hell. Fucking. Yes. As the kiss grew with passion, Collie wound her arms around Jerrie's neck, grabbing on to the hair at the base of her neck in order to keep her close, her skin finally growing warm. She let out a shudder that ran from head to toe as one of Jerry's hands started roaming down her body until it stopped to squeeze her behind in a way that made Collie grow damp in a way that had nothing to do with the rain.

A car honking startled Collie out of Jerry's embrace before hands could do anymore wandering.

"NOW A CAR PASSES?!" Collie angrily shouted after the speeding vehicle. In response Jerry just let out a loud laugh, relief spelled out on her face.

"I was so worried about you. Are you okay!? Is Lottie okay?!" Jerry was shouting over the thunder as she firmly held onto either side of Collie's face.

"Yes, we are both fine. I lost control of the car and went into the ditch. MawMaw is waiting to be rescued."

"Well, we better go rescue her then." With a wink, Jerry grabbed Collie's hand and led the way back to the truck. With one more kiss that quickly morphed from a quick peck to a deeper more meaningful one, they were on their way to where the car was.

***

As the Fourth of July quickly came and passed, Collie found herself pacing her bedroom one night, indecision driving her mad. Things had grown awkward ever since Collie had ran the car into the ditch. They still followed their usual routine, but the casual talking and flirting had fallen to dwindled. Even Collie had felt herself close up, and If she was being honest with herself, it was because she was scared as hell. What had started out as a schoolgirl crush had turned into full on adult feelings. She couldn't remember the last time she liked someone this much, and the fact that she was due to return home in two weeks? It left a sick feeling of unease in her belly. She loved New York. She loved living next door to her best friend and only a couple blocks away from her parents. She wasn't sure though that returning home was the right decision. Actually, her gut was yelling at her that it was the absolute worst decision to make. But to permanently move to Georgia because of a girl she had only known for a few months? That had to be even crazier, right? *Jerry hasn't even asked you to stay. For all you know, you were just a summer fling.* As the ugly inner demon called Anxiety woke up, she flopped down onto the bed. As she stared up at the ceiling fan whose sole purpose was to make noise and blow hot air around, a light knocking sound floated into the air.

"Come on in." She looked over, expecting to see her MawMaw, but it was Jerry who nervously walked in. She didn't say anything, but walked over and assumed the same position, close enough to Collie that their arms were brushing. "Are you going to say something or…?" Was Collie being a bit rude? Yup, but hello unhealthy coping mechanisms.

"Don't leave." Jerry spoke so quietly that Collie could barely make out the words. She slowly sat up, and watched as Jerry followed suit.

"What did you say?" Collie's voice came out in a wisp of air. Astonishment coloring her face.

"You heard me. Stay. Please." Jerry's eyes implored Collie, who felt a pulling on her heart stronger than anything she had ever felt before. Her heart was pounding wildly, and she had to pinch herself to make sure she hadn't fallen asleep. *This could be a dream. Yes, I am totally dreaming, right?*

"I didn't think you would want me to stay. You've just seemed so… distant lately."

"Listen, I know things have been awkward between us lately. I was upset that you were leaving, and instead of making sure that every last minute counted, I got childish and tried to ignore whatever is growing between us. But I can't ignore this. It's too real… Also… Lottie smacked me upside the head and told me I was being an idiot." Jerry grinned ruefully, and as much as Collie tried to keep a straight face, she let out a little chuckle.

"That… doesn't actually surprise me…"

"So? Stay?"

"Oh I don't know. What if this… Thing… between us doesn't work out?" Collie waved her hand between the two of them, as if Jerry wouldn't know what the "thing" was.

"And what if it does?" Jerry was serious as she responded. Grabbing Collie's hand, Jerry placed it on her heart. "My heart is all yours. You just have to take it. So tell me Las, will you stay?"

If anything could make Collie melt, that was it.

Leaning forward, she placed a soft kiss on Jerry's lips before giving her response.
"Yes."

A Summer Solstice Mistake
Carrie Humphrey

Like magic to a starved soul, summer showers wash over all it touches, quenching the thirst of a parched Earth.

Too bad it also brought out the worst in what nature could, and had, created.

Demons liked the rain, it hid their smell, or so they thought.

Nastia squinted her eyes and looked towards the tree line that bordered her property. A demon was there, pacing like a trapped animal ready for a kill, wearing a line into the dirt as it tried and failed to move forward with its quest. Despite the rain, she could smell him long before she could see him in her scope. Having demon blood running through her veins helped.

He could pace all he wanted. He would not break through her magic, no matter how strong he assumed he was.

Part of her wanted to taunt the demon. To walk right up to him, stick out her tongue and offer her neck. She'd find a sick pleasure in watching the crazed beast crash into the barrier that protected her from him. Rather protected him from her. Except, it didn't really protect him. Anything she threw his way would penetrate her magic and hit its target. Every single time.

Instead of giving in to a child's temptation of taunting, she laid on her roof, her body pressed flush to the shingles. The butt of her assault rifle sat against her shoulder, the pressure of its weight a friendly reminder that she was the deadliest force between the two.

Granted, she didn't need the rifle to kill. It was just more fun.

Closing her right eye, seeming to favor her left side tonight, she peered through her scope at her target, watching the demon rage as it felt dawn pressing into the horizon. His time was almost up and she imaged that if he returned to ground without confirmation of a kill, well, he would have had a terrible day.

As it stood, his day was about to get worse. So, what she was about to do was a mercy. Not that she cared. This was her job, what she was bred to do. And she did it very well.

Releasing a steading breath, she pulled the trigger. In silence, the poisoned bullet flew and hit its target in the chest, dropping the demon before he had the time to realize something was wrong.

She watched the look of shock cross his face before his body began to wither in pain. He opened his mouth to scream and when no sound came out; he disappeared in a pop, leaving nothing in his wake aside from a cloud of gray smoke that drifted away with the calming breeze.

Sighing, she pushed herself to sit and did a sweep of her property, checking to see that she was alone again. With the dawn approaching, the likelihood of a demon, or hunter, being out was slim, but it had happened. The sun was as efficient a killer as she.

Yawning, she flipped the safety on her rifle, shouldered it, and stood. Walking to the edge of the roof, she stepped off and dropped to the ground, landing with hardly a sound.

Taking one last look around, satisfied that she was alone, she turned towards the door and entered her home, taking care to reinforce the magic that protected her property and everything within.

Nodding to herself, she walked to her safe and tucked in her rifle next to the other toys she had collected over the years. Some were factory bought, some were custom made, and all were prized possessions that she kept under lock, key, and magic.

Yawning again, she wished she could lie down and rest, but knew rest would not come. Something had keyed her up, and despite the clean kill, her nerves were on edge. The steady patter of the rain was comforting, soothing, yet she needed to keep moving, driving by the need to seek out something she couldn't identify.

Flipping on the coffee maker, she grabbed her phone and propped her body against the counter. Nothing new was happening in the social media world; there was no recent emails or messages, and for the first time in a long time, there were no new targets waiting for elimination in her queue. And yes, she had an app for that.

Weird. Setting the phone down, she grabbed a mug and filled it to the brim, taking a sip and cherishing the burn as it hit her throat.

Her genetic makeup meant that hot coffee burned, but it was a pain she enjoyed, not something discomforting. Thanks to excellent genes, there was a lot she could do with minor side effects.

Demon hunter. Exterminator. Executioner. Those were just a few names she had been called over the last few thousand years. All were true. All were what she was bred to do. Between the blood in her body that ranged from demon to vampire, some shifter, and a little god, she was damn near impossible to kill. A weapon with a conscience. Well, a little one. She was a Night Assassin, long lived and long feared.

She was also tired.

The job was great for the first few hundred years. The hunt, thrilling. After all, that was why she was created, to hunt and kill and be damn good at both. Among her kind, she was the best and had done what was asked of her, without question, for thousands of years. The rush of adrenalin when she marked her kill and the flair of recognition in the eyes of the damned when she came to claim her due, was a high she could find nowhere else.

But when the day was done, and she retired to her place in the woods, she was tired. She was bored, maybe. Friends were few, lovers even less. Her mind was just. . .tired.

Others like her kept in touch, but they had their own lives to go back to. She was alone and to anyone else; she wanted it that way. To anyone else, she had always been a loner and would always be. Deep in her cold heart, she yearned to come home and not be the only person in residence.

That was a reality that wasn't meant to be. One she wouldn't allow. There was too much heartache to be had and it would affect her hunt, her ability to think clearly.

Stepping out of the house and onto her back porch, she turned her body to face the east, watching the sun as it rose in the sky. The air was warm, the rain having stopped, and summer in full bloom as the sky began to brighten with a new day.

Lost in her thoughts, she watched the sun crest into the horizon, until a strange noise caught her attention. When it happened again, she grinned and looked down. "Oh, all right, we'll eat."

She was so lonely she was talking to her body, as if it could talk back.

Heading back into the house, she changed her clothes into someone a little more normal. Her hunting style had always been black leather, as much of it as she could find. Besides it being like a second skin, enabling her to move freely, she liked the feel of the smooth texture against her bare skin. If she had to wear clothes, in the very distant past it wasn't a requirement, then leather was her go to.

Now, in modern days, if she wore leather out in public, she'd get more attention that she needed. Humans were incredibly misguided in their opinions on who should wear what and how they should wear it. She didn't need the extra attention, so her favorite fabric was hidden away for special missions and occasions.

Despite it being summer, she grabbed a pair of jeans and a long sleeve black shirt. It was easier to hide weapons under, which she did as she strapped a knife to her thigh, one to her forearm and grabbed her boots that also had pockets for more knives. She was just going to the local diner, so there was no need to grab a gun. The knives should be plenty.

Her own body was a weapon, if needed. At will, her hands could become claws, her teeth into fangs and her body could produce a poison that would drop almost any type of creature that could threaten her.

She wasn't immortal, but she was damn hard to take down. God help anyone that tried because she would take them to hell with her. Of course, hell would spit her back out, not needing her kind to take over down there.

Making her way back to the kitchen, she filled a food bowl that sat on the ground, cleaned out a water dish and filled it with part ice and part water, just the way her puppy liked it. Puppy was using the term lightly. Alex was as old as she was, and a product of Greek mythology made real. A hell hound, decedent of Cerberus, Alex was one of a litter of twenty that had been auctioned off at a price that made her skin crawl. That alone had her taking the job to kill the breeder and rescue the pups, keeping one for herself as payment.

Putting her pointer fingers in her mouth, she whistled loudly then paused, waiting. Alex came bounding in from the guest room, his multiple heads up, tongues out, as he cornered her in the kitchen and licked her outstretched hand.

She had learned long ago that as cute as Alex was, and as loyal as he tried to be, she was to never get her face near any of his. There was a scar above her left eye, hidden in her brow, that proved how dangerous he was.

"I'm going out, you be good," she said, petting to each of Alex's heads. "And do not bring another live animal in this house. If you are going to hunt, do it outside, and keep the blood off my hardwood floor. Do we remember how long that took to clean last time?"

Alex sunk his heads to the ground and shook his heads in a slow no. She smiled and gave him another pet. "Guard the place and I'll bring you back some bacon." Her dog perked up, tongues back out, and wagged his tail viciously. That was another part of the dog you never wanted to be near. His tail was thick as braided rope and she'd seen him decapitate humans with one swish.

Grinning, she walked out of the house and to her jeep. With the rise of technology, she had to admit that the development of vehicles was one of her favorite accomplishments. She did not possess the ability to move with just a thought, like some of her brethren, so the addition of wheels was a nice advancement for her.

Throwing the jeep in drive, she tore out of her driveway and headed for town. It wouldn't take long to get to the diner, and with the windows down and the breeze dancing over her skin, she slowed and took her time.

For so many years she fought on autopilot. So many years spent racing from job to job, doing what needed to be done, what was programed in the core of her being to do. For the first time she found herself in a position where she could stop and smell the roses, as they say.

It was an odd sensation. She felt like she was cheating somehow, like she wasn't living up to expectations. But that wasn't accurate. Her prey, those that would seek to destroy what the Gods created, numbers had diminished.

Which meant her jobs were slowing down. She felt like the Gods were even going as far as to forget her kind even existed. It had been a gradual decline over the past thousand years. There was chatter about what would happen to them when the last creature fell, but no one knew when that would be and no one wanted to admit to being useless.

As for her, she felt the decline, but there was something more. A nagging in her gut that despite numbers going down, something was on the rise. From the depths of whatever hell that was in charge, something was brewing.

Shaking off the unease she felt, she focused back on the road only to realize that she was already at the diner. Pulling into the grass in the back, she parked and made her way towards the entrance.

Just as she was about to touch the door handle, a

chill danced across her skin. She was not alone. And it had nothing to do with the humans that were fluttering around. They didn't hit her radar.

No, there was someone else here, something like her.

Closing her eyes for a moment, she collected her own calm before entering the diner. Whoever was here, they hadn't attacked, which was promising. Or stupid. Time would tell.

"Nastia!" a bubbly young waitress called out, waving her over to a booth in the far corner, one she always used when she visited. "I had a feeling you would be in today."

"And here I am," she said with a smile. The waitress, Elli, had a sixth sense about things that wasn't normal, and with it came an aura of caution, which was why Nastia liked her. She was brilliantly smart and only working the diner to pay for college until something else came her way. "How's your summer going?"

"All work and no play, you know how it is. You want your usual?" Elli asked, taking a pencil and pad of paper out of her apron and began to write before Nastia could reply.

"Of course, and make it a double side of bacon to go."

"I wish you'd bring that dog in here so we can properly spoil him," Elli laughed as she pocketed her notepad and grabbed the coffee pot, filling her cup.

Nastia would love to bring Alex, but the several heads thing would scare off a few people. "Maybe someday."

Elli grinned and left to put her order in. Still feeling the presence of something not human, Nastia looked around for the source of the unease she was feeling. She couldn't see anyone, which didn't mean much. All that meant was that whoever was stalking her had magic, and was hiding.

Breakfast went by in relative silence. Few people came up to her to make small talk, and for that she was grateful. She wasn't much in the mood to focus on keeping her conversation human when something entirely not was watching.

Whoever it was, wasn't coming in for a kill, yet. This was the track-your-prey-stage. The learn the movements and locations your victim like to visit, stage. She should know, it was her job to do the same. Most of the time she got bored and went ahead and just took out her target, cleaning up the mess afterwards. Sometimes that got her in trouble, but most of the time no one ever realized just how much she broke protocol.

Paying the bill and leaving a hefty tip, she grabbed her to-go bag and made her way back out to the jeep. She remained casual, never changing her body language to suggest that she knew someone was out there. The moment she alerted them; they would attack. She was sure of it.

If that person was smart, though, they'd know that the tables could turn in an instant. No one took her as a target without understanding just how deadly she was. And if they did, they deserved to die.

The drive home was quick and when she walked in the door, she was greeted with the house-shaking patter of Alex as he skidded to a halt before her, heads up and waiting for the treats he knew she had.

Smiling, she dished out the bacon to all the mouths, being sure to avoid his teeth. After some scratches and love, Alex dashed off to his bed in the guest room. It was time for his mid-morning nap.

Any other day, and she'd lay down to rest. But knowing that someone was tracking her kept her from even thinking about shutting her eyes.

Breathing out a frustrated breath, because it would be a long day, she went about doing all the things she normally avoided. She caught up on laundry, cleaned the bathrooms, weeded her garden while avoiding the snapping jaws of the plants that were alive, read a book, and made a stew for dinner that she could freeze for the next few weeks.

Domesticated life was never something she strived to achieve, but in modern days when her jobs were winding down, she found it wasn't so bad. The invention of microwaves, and washing machines helped significantly. Still, she'd rather be hunting and killing things. Some traits ingrained in your body just never went away.

Hours passed, and whoever was tracking her hadn't left the edge of her property, nor had he made a move in any direction. She had already pinpointed his exact location and had been checking from time to time to see if he had moved. Frustration that this party hadn't even started, she wandered to her room to retrieve more knives, strapping them in place. If the hunter would not come to her, she was just going to have to go to him.

Under the cover of night, she left the house and ventured out onto her property, her body drawn to the place where the hunter was hiding. Once into the trees, she climbed up, and silently jumped from branch to branch to get to her destination.

There. Laying flat on his stomach, his own weapon primed for a shot, the demon who'd been watching her showed no sign that he knew she was now above him.

His mistake.

With grace, she dropped, straddling the man's back. Following the movement downward, she put her knees on the dirt and her elbow in the dip at the base of his neck. If she applied enough pressure with where she was positioned, she could pop his head right off.

"What are you doing here?" she asked calmly. It didn't skip her notice that the man below her hadn't even twitched at her sudden appearance.

"Looking for you." His voice was powerful, edged with humor, and threatened to melt her insides with its smooth tone and slight hint of an accent she couldn't place.

"Why?"

"A job."

"From who?"

"My employer."

"Who is?"

"To remain anonymous." The silken edge of his tone vibrated through her body and because of her position, she was beginning to feel uncomfortable, in an entirely inappropriate way.

If he was refusing to say who the job belonged to, it was probably one of the Titans. They were the only Gods who were consistently putting hits out on her kind. They were never able to understand how lower Gods could have created such accurate and deadly killing machines. "Which Titan?" Thousands of years and they still couldn't leave well enough alone.

The man beneath her chuckled, the sound vibrating from his body and into hers, causing another reaction she was not expecting. A wash of desire slammed into her and a moan left her lips before she could stop it.

In the next instant, before she could think to react, the man below her lifted his body from the ground, flipping them both over, catching her off guard. Now she was on her back with his powerful legs straddling her stomach, his elbow now pressing into her throat, and a blade nipping at her side.

Oh, he was good. Looking up, she sucked in a shocked breath, this time at the familiarity of the face that looked down on her. She'd never seen him before, but knew his features well. Olive skin, sharp jaw, defined nose and piercing red eyes; he was every bit the demon she expected him to be and something more. Something, unique.

He was bone chillingly handsome, his voice smooth and calculated, his moves precise and practiced. If he was younger than a thousand, she'd be shocked.

Swallowing, feeling the pressure of his elbow on her throat, she smiled and raised a brow. "You're good," she commented before bucking her body and twisting, grabbing his hand with the knife and bringing them both to vertical. Keeping his hand steady, and the knife within a centimeter from her vital organs, she pulled her own weapon and positioned it to mirror his own. "But I'm better."

The demon in front of her smiled all the way up to his eyes, which flared with lust. Another wave of desire slammed into her, this time causing her body to sway, but not enough to lose her focus.

Something wasn't right. He should not be having this effect on her. No one should.

Between one blink in the next, before her brain could process what was happening, the demon crushed his lips to hers, his tongue darting out, demanding entrance into her body.

Moaning at the sudden change of stance, her body accepted him, the desire that had overwhelmed her was now seeking to quench its thirst. This wasn't right. This wasn't. . . her thoughts trailed off as his palm gripped her side, pulling her body flush against his own. "I thought," she said and paused as his mouth continued to demand attention from her own. "Thought you were here to kill me."

"It can wait," he groaned, the sound animalistic and needy.

This wasn't like her. Every move she made was pre-planned. Thought out. Yet, as this man's mouth devoured her own, she couldn't stop her body's reaction to him. There was something, a nagging sensation in the back of her mind, that knew why, but lust took over and all she knew was that they were both wearing too many clothes and there were too many weapons still in play.

"This will not work with your knife at my side." Her voice sounded foreign, breathless and heady.

"Drop yours first." The man's hand was steady at her hip while the other trailed upwards, taking her breast into his grasp and squeezing, bring a strangled gasp from her throat.

Wild with a need that hit her out of the blue, she dropped her weapon. Seconds later, she listened as metal met metal, his own knife dropping. The hand that had been occupied, found her other breast and gave it the same attention. Crying out, she racked her nails down his back, desperate to feel his skin. Desperate for, more.

She didn't even know his name. "Nathan," he muttered into her mouth as he nipped at her lip, answering her unasked question.

Something in his name brought a wave of warning, but the feeling was fleeting, the heat of their combined desire outweighing any red flag that may be flying in her mind.

Needing to feel his skin, she grabbed the hem of his shirt and tossed it over his head and off into the distance. He followed suit, shedding her shirt and pulling her close. The quick glimpse of his body revealed hard muscles, lines of scars that marked years of hunting, and a whole lot of delicious that she wanted to explore with her tongue.

Nathan's hands tugged at the waist of her jeans, causing her to flush with anticipation.

Her thoughts were getting muddled, but for some reason the overwhelming urge to know what day it was flared to life. Something about this specific day that ran the gambit of warnings in her mind, but the blinding passion she felt overrode conscience thought.

"Shit," she ground out as Nathan's hand found its way to the junction between her thighs. He nipped at her shoulder, tracing a line with his lips up her neck and back to her mouth.

She couldn't think as he continued to explore her skin. She needed to stop. She needed to think.

Something wasn't right here. Their reaction to each other wasn't natural.

Just as she was about to open her mouth to protest, Nathan bit into her neck, just above the vein that would leak a facet had he gotten down that far. She knew the moment her blood hit his mouth; his entire body froze as a moan of pure ecstasy left his throat.

Like a rubber band snapping into place, the things she was trying to remember cleared through her jumbled thoughts, causing a jolt of alarm to push her body away from his.

Breathing heavily, she looked at Nathan with wide eyes. His own breathing was labored, he looked like sex in a pair of jeans and he held a gaze that peered directly into her soul.

Focusing on calming herself down, she listened to the cicadas and frogs sing their nightly songs while nocturnal animals went about their business like nothing was happing around them. Not too far away, an owl called out and the small sound of its dinner scurried across a patch of dead leaves.

The breeze of a summer night danced over her warmed skin, dotting her body in a blanket of goosebumps.

All these things calmed her, collected her thoughts and led her towards figuring out what the hell was going on. "What day is it?"

"The twentieth of June," Nathan answered, his voice as strong as the muscles straining under his control. His hands were balled into fists at his sides and there was a tick in his jaw, like he wanted to say something, do something, but was holding back.

"The twentieth," she whispered, then sucked in a sharp breath. "Fuck. It's the summer solstice." Shit, that was not good.

A slow smile spread across his face, like he understood her fear. But he was a demon. He couldn't possibly understand what she feared. "So?"

"Do you have any idea what you have done?" she seethed, her lust for him turning into an emotion she understood. Anger.

"Played with my food?" he said with a shrug, furthering her irritation as she tried to ignore the way his words made her want to get naked while also being furious that she allowed this to happen.

"This did not happen," she shot out, looking around for her shirt and her knife. She didn't need them; they were just a distraction for her eyes.

"I'm going to beg to differ, Night Assassin." Nathan's voice surrounded her, snapping her gaze back to his. He held her there, locked in a moment she feared she could not break.

Desperate to move, she darted for her weapon and froze from his hand cupped her cheek, bringing her gently back to standing before him. Growling, she grabbed his wrist, ducked under his hold and twisted his arm to behind his back. Pulling the knife that was strapped to her forearm, she let the tip bite at the man's throat. He never moved, never took a breath, which just pissed her off even more. "I will not be bound to the likes of you."

She could feel him grin right before he leaned forward into her blade. When a drop of blood bloomed on his skin, her body roared to life, demanding more. It took her godlike strength not to go for his vein, the one she could see pulsing steady and strong at his neck. Shit.

Pulling her blade away from his body, she stepped back, turned, and bolted.

"You can't run away from this," he called out. Something in the way he spoke, the confidence he wore, told her he knew what was happening. How he'd come to that knowledge, she was not going to wait around to find out. She needed to be gone, fifteen minutes ago.

"Wanna bet?" she called out and took off, crossing the safety of her magic, never slowing. As she ran, an ancient chant, one she had been born with ingrained in her mind.

"On the day the sun shines the longest and the moon's glow fills the night sky, the soul will bind to that with which it seeks. To bring two souls together is to find your greatest treasure and your dire weakness. Watch the Summer Solstice, for love and lust become the same and two lives become one."

She was a Night Assassin, a genesis one, and she had just made a brutal mistake.

Summer Wings
K.R. Cervantez

Drake

"It says here that she was second in hand to hand combat in her training." I grinned as I flipped through the paperwork. The fan blew hot summer air around the room only making things feel hotter. I tipped back the chip bag to my mouth, emptying it of the crumbs.

"Drake," Garrett said, he limped over, still bandaged and recovering from our last mission. I knew he hated being hurt.

"Number one in defense and support. She's saved a bunch of people. And she's a great healer." I kept reading. "Trained with several different weapons. I wasn't usually easily impressed but this was something.

"Drake." Garrett said again.

"Woah, she's a nymphacera! A butterfly nymph. I thought they went into hiding when their people were being hunted for their wings. This is incredible!" I chuckled. I couldn't believe my luck. After requesting a new partner from the agency, I expected some rookie but this woman sounded badass and experienced. As much as

I'd miss Garrett on missions, I knew he had to heal. Although, maybe this nymphacera could speed up the healing process....

"Drake!" Garrett grabbed my shoulder. "She's here. Waiting for you in the front room." I tossed the paperwork onto my desk and grabbed my package of jerky. I gave Garrett a wink as I left. This mission would be easy considering all the skills my new partner had. Or at least it should go smoothly.

I stopped in the doorway with a frown. The woman in question was crouched next to the door. Her breathtaking wings fluttered in agitation the bits of blue, purple and pink all splashed together making her wings look exotic. They were iridescent and shimmery. I could understand why nymphacera's were hunted for their wings. My own wings - currently tucked into the slits of my back - were dull and bulky compared to hers. I started to say something to let her know I was there but I heard her soft voice as she spoke.

"Oh, I'm so sorry little guy." Her voice cracked. I frowned at the distress in her tone. "I didn't see you. Oh God... I'm so sorry." She actually sounded like she was close to tears. I leaned forward to see her scooping up a squished spider and sighed. Maybe this was a different nymphacera because there was no way this was the badass woman I'd just read about.

I cleared my throat, "Are you Kallima?" She spun to face me. The ache in my chest hit hard and warmth spread throughout my body. My heart thumped harshly against my ribcage. The smell of summer rains and freshly baked cherry blossoms wafted around me. My body reacted as if I were a young teenage boy again. I knew this feeling although, I had never experienced it before. Garrett talked about it when he met his Rena. An imprinting bond. Kallima, was my mate. My intended and I was suddenly scared to death about the mission.

Everything happened so fast as I took in the rest of her appearance. She was extraordinary. She had mismatched eyes, one pink and one purple. Her hair was the color of cinnamon, pulled back into a long ponytail. She stood, cradling the damn dead spider in the palm of her hand, tears still pooling in her eyes. She wore a dress of all things and sandals. Definitely not mission appropriate attire. She looked delicate, soft and nothing at all like someone who passed her training as the second ranked with unlocked potential. She blinked at me, her eyes clearing.

"Oh." She breathed. "You're…. Scared. And disappointed…" I rubbed the ache in my chest resisting the sudden urge to hold this stranger.

Kallima

Drake Mendez towered over me. His aura swirled around him; the navy blue and gray circling each over in an exotic dance. There was the softest pink mixed in as well that didn't quite make sense to me.

I still held the poor little spider I had crushed in my rush to get out of the heat. Drake hadn't said anything else as he stared at me. I pulled my wings behind me thinking maybe they were distracting him. He closed his eyes, clutching the bag of jerky he had in his hand tightly as he took a deep breath.

"Are you Kallima Hart?" He asked again. I nodded slowly and swallowed hard. I didn't know why he was so disappointed. I'd sent in my resumé in; surely he knew how qualified I was for the job.

"I am." I said. He ran a hand through his hair, his fingers catching on a few tangles. His gaze raked over me and the navy in his aura faded a little as violet began to bleed through My cheeks heated as I knew what that color meant... I had seen this aura before when people looked at me. It wasn't uncommon, as people were attracted to my wings, but this was the first time a heated gaze affected me. Drake was handsome, tall, with hard earned muscles and deep gray eyes that almost looked silver. I shuddered at the sudden ache in my body. I couldn't see my own aura, but I knew it would be violet too. I moved closer and a different kind of heat enveloped me. This one felt soothing and safe. I smelled lemons and lavender, the scent drawing me in. I had the urge to wrap my arms around this man and I didn't know why.

"Put the spider down and come on then. We have a lot to talk about before we get started on the mission." He said. His voice hitched a bit as I gently placed the spider in the potted plant by the door. It seemed like the best option. "And please tell me you brought your gear." I flashed him a smile and grabbed my bag. I hefted it to my shoulder with a grunt.

"I got it. My trainer told me about the mermaids. I have some ideas written down." I said. Drake raised his eyebrows but didn't say anything. I followed him into the back room.

A man sat in a chair by the window. I could see the thick bandages under his shirt and his aura was the sickly green of pain. I knew he was Garrett, Drake's ex-partner. I had seen his file before I came here; he'd been mauled by a Werebear during a mission.

"Oh my..." I said softly. I started for him, reaching a hand out. "Is there something I can do? I can heal really well. I know that your injuries are pretty bad but I can do something." My fingertips tingled and Drake let out a low growl as Garrett smiled.

"Don't touch him!" He snapped. I backpedaled and looked over at him, confused. Surely, he knew that I wouldn't hurt him. Garrett looked from Drake to me and his smile turned into a smirk.

"I see now." He chuckled. He winked at me, earning him another growl from Drake. "Don't worry sweetheart. I have to go see my healer in a bit anyway. Thank you though." He stood up and grabbed his crutch. "You two have fun!" He laughed and patted his shoulder. "Good luck my friend." He left, hobbling out.

"Come on. We have work to do." Drake said. He snatched a water bottle and tossed it to me. I caught it easily and sat down next to him.

Drake

I didn't want this. Well that wasn't exactly true. I had wanted a woman, and I wanted a family but I didn't have time for this. Kallima was gorgeous and so full of life. I wanted to call the agency and ask for another partner. This need to protect her was strong and new to me. And the fact that the thought of her touching my best friend to heal him had nearly sent me into a rage, unsettled me.

Then there was her scent. As she leaned over to grab her bag again, the smell had lingered in the air. My body had heated about another hundred degrees and demanded that I kiss her. Claim her.

"You're a gargoyle, right?" She asked. She flicked her gaze to me as she gathered her papers. I nodded and took a drink of water. "Can I see your wings?" I choked and coughed the liquid out of my throat with a frown.

"Why?" I asked, genuinely confused.

"I always heard they were unique." She shrugged. She chewed on her lip, oblivious to the effect it had on me.

"Let's just get to work. We are on a time crunch." She nodded and passed over her papers. I paused, and couldn't help but smile. She had color coated her plan and ideas. My name was in the corner, each letter in a different color. She had even added a smiley face in the opposite corner.

"The mermaids are being killed for their scales. I'm thinking it's for selling on the Black Market." She said as she ran her fingers over the words on her own paper.

"My guess is that it's the Snake Shifters. They've been pretty active in the market lately." I told her as she nodded in agreement. "I say that we stake out their Den and see what happens." I scanned the paper she gave me. She had thought of the Snake Shifters as suspects.

"No. That would waste time and put the mermaids in danger. I say we go to the beach!" She grinned at me as I raised my eyebrows at her. "I can rent us a yurt and we can keep watch." I had no argument for that. Staking out the Den would be easier, but the beach might just be quicker and it had nothing to do with the thought of seeing my new mate in a swimsuit.

"Sailor's Cove was hit a few weeks back. It's a good chance that they will try there again." I said. Again, I looked over the paper she gave me. Sailor's Cove was written there along with some other beaches. Kallima was smart and calculating, I had to admit. She smiled widely.

She stood and grabbed her phone. "I'll get us a yurt." I swore under my breath. Spending the night in a yurt with this woman would be torture. I didn't know how I was going to tell her I had imprinted on her.

Nymphacera's were independent by nature, free spirited and she might not like being tied down.

Kallima

Drake pulled up to the yurt and put the jeep in park. His aura was dark with worry, and there was still the pink that confused me. We had loaded it up like we were on vacation, though I had seen Drake pack weapons. I'd wanted to protest but he had seemed so tense, plus this was still a mission and we had to prepare.

I jumped out of the jeep. "Let's unpack and hit the beach." I grabbed my bag. Drake chuckled softly as he began to unload. The yurt was small but comfortable and it overlooked the beach perfectly. It didn't take long to unload. I watched Drake set up security cameras and surveillance equipment. He moved quickly and efficiently and he always seemed to have a different snack in his mouth every time I looked at him. It made me smile; the guy sure likes to snack.

He already wore his swim shorts and a tank top, and I swear I was going to start drooling. He snacked a lot, yes but he sure didn't look like it. I wondered again about his wings. I'd heard that each Gargoyles wings were different. I was curious about him. I had been since I'd read his file, but now seeing him in person, something about him drew me in.

He leaned down to untangle a wire, and I walked over. "Need any help?" I asked. I touched his arm and he jumped, almost dropping the carrot stick from his mouth. The violet in his aura grew quickly. Did he desire me, as I did him? He glanced at me.

"Just go get changed so we can scout the beach." He grumbled. He gave me a soft smile and jerked his head towards the bathroom. I paused, watching him fiddle with the wires before grabbing them from him.

"I'll change in a bit." I said, pulling at the tangled mess. "I figure that whoever is going after the mermaids won't strike during the day while all the tourists are out and about, but they may be watching and planning." I said. He nodded, grabbing a candy bar. He offered me half, which I graciously accepted.

"I also want to check out the lighthouse." He said. I felt him watching me and the ache in my chest and body grew. I untangled the wires and plugged them in. I turned and smiled, eating the offered chocolate.

"Now I'll get ready." I said. I booped his nose and made my way to the bathroom. I took this opportunity to try to calm myself down. I couldn't stop thinking about his arms wrapped around me, or lips on mine. I knew he felt the same. I saw it in his aura but the mission came first and besides, we barely knew each other. Maybe after we figured out who was killing the mermaids, we could talk about this mutual desire.

I splashed water on my face and changed into my swimsuit and put on my crocheted cover but I didn't feel any calmer. I stepped out of the bathroom and froze. Drake was staring at me. His whole Aura was violet, but I didn't need to see it to know how much he wanted me.

Drake

She should not have been this beautiful. I should not want her this bad. And she should not be looking at me like that; it didn't help this raw desire I felt for her. She wore a rainbow swimsuit cover and she had braided her hair back in two braids.

Her eyes were wide, her pupils blown. Her mismatched eyes mesmerized me. Her wings fluttered behind her, nervously. I wanted to touch them; I wanted to bring out my own wings so she could touch mine. I battled with the urge to pin her to the wall and kiss her until we were both breathless. Her eyes flickered to my lips and I knew she thought the same. I swallowed hard.

"We need to…" she said softly. I nodded, moving closer to her. I pinched the end of one braid.

"Get started on the mission, I know." I closed my eyes as her scent enveloped me. She put a hand on my chest, moving closer. She looked up at me, licking her lips.

"I don't think you're thinking about the mission." She breathed. I shook my head. The urge was so much stronger now. I growled softly, leaning forward. How would she taste? How would she sound?

My computer beeped then, alerting me that the motion sensor detected something coming closer. Kallima jerked away, a blush coloring her cheeks. She smiled up at me, her eyes still as sensual as before. I sighed heavily and we both went to check the camera, though it was just a tourist with a metal detector.

"We should head to the beach." Kallima said as she picked up her beach bag. I smiled softly as I grabbed my own things.

We made our way to the beach. It was crowded with tourists and people on summer vacation. I spotted a group of Elves playing Volleyball and little werewolves playing in the sand. There was a group of mermaids laying in the waves, playing with human children and keeping watch for sharks. Mermaids were great Life Guards. I loved that we didn't have to hide from the humans anymore, although we did have to be cautious at times.

Kallima laid out a blanket and shrugged off her swimsuit cover. I swore softly; this was definitely torture. I expected a colorful bikini but this one was simple and pale gray. She was absolutely stunning and I could feel people staring at her. I wanted to cover her up and hide her from every desired gaze but then again, I wanted to show everyone that she was mine. But she wasn't mine, not yet.

She slapped a bottle of sunscreen in my hand. "Can you get my back?" She asked. I nodded, already squeezing the lotion into my hand, eager to put my hands on her. Her wings flittered with excitement.

"We are supposed to be staying focused." I chided gently as I rubbed her shoulders. "Not having fun." She let out a breathless sigh which made my trunks feel much tighter.

"I am focused. I saw twelve people wearing the same purple sun hat. The three mermaid children have been bringing crabs up to show the fairy children. And the woman with the pineapple drink at the snack bar has been staring at you since we got here." She said so easily. I blinked, utterly impressed by how perceptive she was. All this time, I thought that she was aloof but just acting?

I worked my hands between her wings but froze. She stiffened too, probably knowing what I'd seen. She had deep scarring by her wings. Jagged, puffy scars that still looked painful. There was even a spot on her wings. I felt the growl rumble in my chest as I spun her around.

"Someone hurt you." I snapped. "They tried to take your wings." The sudden fury I felt almost scared me. I wanted to track down the bastard that did this and make him wish he were dead. This rage was new to me.

The color drained from her face and she dropped her gaze. She hugged herself, tears filling up her eyes. This was still bothering her. She was upset and I hated it. The need to cheer her up, outweighed the rage. I put a hand on her cheek in a show of comfort and knelt down to turn on the radio, she had packed. I grinned, trying to calm myself down.

"I like this song." She whispered softly. I bobbed my head to the beat.

"So do I." I grinned at her, lip syncing as I played the air guitar. The color returned to her cheeks and she giggled. The tragedy she'd been thinking about, gone for a moment at least. I took her hands and spun her around with a laugh, happy to have taken her mind off it. But I couldn't stop thinking about what could have happened to her. How badly had she been hurt?

I ended our dance as the song changed to another. She was laughing again, and pride filled me. I'd done that. I dumped out my bag of snacks onto the blanket.

"Come on. Let's feast." I said. She plopped down with a grin and patted a spot next to her. My chest ached even more now. This Intended Imprint was strong and I was beginning to like it.

Kallima

I could almost pretend that Drake and I were on a summer vacation together, like everyone else. He was sweet and I was beginning to really like him as a person. I still desired him, and that was only getting stronger but I was also enjoying his company quite a bit.

We walked the shore collecting sea glass. I'd mentioned how I had a collection and Drake jumped up from his mountain of snacks and decided that we would add to my treasures. It was these little details that made being with him so much fun. We hadn't forgotten the mission though, and we were slowly making our way to the lighthouse.

I had hoped he wouldn't see the scars around my wings, but he had and the rage I'd seen in his Aura made me shiver. He'd wanted blood and for some reason it was oddly comforting. The memories had come back and I'd been scared to say anything at first, but now part of me wanted him to know.

"It was four years ago." I started playing with my braid. Drake was scooping through the water to look for more sea glass. He paused for a moment.

"You don't have to talk about it Kalli." He said, he flashed me a smirk as he tossed another blue piece to add to my collection.

"I know, I don't have to." I sighed. "I was going home. I was 24. I shouldn't have been alone; I knew us Butterfly Nymphs were being hunted. I was grabbed and tossed into an alley." I shuddered and stretched my wings. Drake was facing me now, listening to every word with a dark scowl that both scared and excited me. "I fought as best as I could but he had friends and they pinned me down. Thankfully someone had heard me screaming and came but the damage had been done. I was in the hospital for a few days and I still can't fly for long periods of time. But," I took a deep breath. "I joined the agency so that I could save others like me. I hate violence but I want to save people. I want to find out who's killing mermaids and stop them." I finished quickly.

Drake was quiet for a moment, but he moved closer. His warmth spread through me. The deep red of rage was back in his aura but so was a soft blue and the pink. That pink still confused me and I wondered why it was getting bigger. He put his fingers under my chin and tilted my head up.

"I've seen a lot of agents quit after being injured like that. But you decided to join because of what happened and that makes you amazing." I smiled softly and laid my head on his chest. It was weird; we'd only just met that afternoon, but I already felt so connected to him. His arms wound around me in a tender embrace.

We stayed like that for a few moments. The waves lapping at our feet and the setting sun warming our shoulders. The beach was clearing slowly. A few tourists remained, having a bonfire or still swimming in the sea. The mermaids were gone but that didn't mean they weren't still in danger.

"Before, you wanted to see my wings. Do you still wanna see them?" Drake asked. I smiled into his chest and nodded. He chuckled and pulled away. I really liked the tenderness I saw in his eyes. I watched as he pulled his tank top over his head. My fingers itched to trace over his abdomen. He really didn't look like he snacked eighty percent of the time.

After a moment, large leathery wings unfolded from his back and I gasped. My wings were beautiful, sure but his wings were glorious. He stretched them out and I could see just how big they were. The outside of them were dark gray, rough and a little scarred. But the inside was smooth, shades of blue and green swirled around. It made me think of the inside of a geode stone.

I reached out to run my fingers across them but Drake shifted them away from me. "If you touch them, Kalli, I will finish what started in the yurt." Violet once again took over the color of his aura. I felt my cheeks warm and shuddered.

"After the mission then." I said and he gave me a crooked smile in agreement.

"Come on, put on your cardigan and let's go check out the light house." He said. He shifted his wings again and settled them behind him. My own fluttered in excitement.

"It's not a cardigan. It's a crocheted swimsuit cover." I teased as I took the garment from him. He still had his wings out and I didn't want him to put them away. He took my hand, our fingers laced and we started towards the lighthouse again.

We were quiet but content. His hand felt amazing in mine. I could definitely get used to it. Drake was smiling and the summer ocean breeze ruffled his hair, making my heart lurch in my chest. How was he affecting me like this?

We got to the lighthouse; the sun almost set. I could see a few mermaids working the night shift for Ocean Clean Up. I knew they were gathering trash from the ocean and keeping it clean. I smiled up at Drake.

"I'm going to talk with the mermaids and see if they know anything, while you start in the lighthouse." I told him. He gave my hand a squeeze and pressed a soft kiss to my palm.

"Be safe." He said softly. I nodded and watched him walk away for a moment. His wings were still out and I had a feeling that it was for my sake. God he was handsome.

I made my way over the rocky tide pools to the trash chutes. A mermaid and merman were separating the garbage. The mermaid had azure colored hair, pretty and long.

"Hey there." I began. They both stiffened which meant they were probably aware of the murders. "No hey, it's okay. I'm from SPA. I'm here to investigate the murders and keep you safe." The merman backed away from the rocky edge a little. He was shirtless though I knew they were supposed to be wearing uniforms.

"You don't look like you're from the Supernatural Protective Services." He said. The mermaid nodded quickly. I smiled.

"I am and I just want to help." I said. "My partner just went to check out the lighthouse." The guy frowned in thought and the mermaid put her hands on his shoulders.

"We just saw a group of Elves go in there. We were about to report it, since no one is supposed to be trespassing." She said. I blinked, standing up.

The Elves were trespassing. They were here, after hours, where the mermaids worked. It wasn't the Snake Shifters after all. And Drake had just walked in without backup.

"Oh god…" I took off running, calling out a thanks as I left. I skidded to a stop when I got inside. Drake was surrounded and though he was putting up a good fight, he was losing.

Drake

Damn Elves. It was the damn Elves. I cursed myself for not seeing it sooner. Pain exploded behind my eyes and one Elf landed a solid blow to my nose. I felt the bones crunching and I stumbled back. Two other guys caught my arms and though I struggled, I couldn't stop the blows from coming. They were wailing on me, not taking any chances. Not giving me a chance to fight back. I kicked and punched when I could, fighting to get my bearings again.

"Drake!" She cried out and my chest lurched. I groaned, fighting harder now. I had to protect her. I watched her lunge at the nearest Elf, throwing herself onto his back. I kicked out a leg, snapping someone's bones but I was still outnumbered.

The Elf threw Kalli off him. I heard her cry out in pain and I growled loudly, but another fist connected with my temple. She screamed again and all I could do was watch her. Tears streamed down her cheeks as she fought to stand. I didn't see the knife, but I sure as hell felt it. Blood bubbled up in my throat. Kalli screamed again. She was on her feet again, but my vision was fading.

I didn't understand what was happening. Not at first at least. Kallima's eyes began to glow. The pink and purple, bleeding into each other. Her hair flew around her face and her hands sparked.

One by one the Elves began to drop. A misty light flew from them to Kallima's hands. Tears streaked down her cheeks. She stumbled back once the last elf fell. She whimpered a little and opened her hands. Tiny butterflies of light floated away from her. Souls. She had taken their souls.

My eyes shut then, but I smiled. My mate would be okay.

Kallima

His flesh began to weave together. I was exhausted. Sucking out the souls of the Elves should have killed me. Believe me, I hurt so bad that I wanted to die. But Drake... Drake needed me. He was dying. His blood soaked my hands and I couldn't stop crying.

"Please don't." I sobbed. I pushed myself, healing more of his wounds. His eyes fluttered open and he gasped for breath. The knife wound, almost healed.

"K..Kalli..." he croaked. "You healed me?" I nodded fast, smiling and laughing through my tears. He smiled weakly. His eyes fluttered but he put a hand on my cheek. "My mate."

"Mate?" I asked, still smiling. I hurt. I hurt so bad, but Drake was alive. He would be okay.

"Yeah... first...time I saw you... I imprinted on you. You're my mate. You just.. have to accept it." He said. I smiled wide. I crushed my lips to his and he groaned. The kiss was wild and untamed. Our tongues dueled and he wound his arms around me, dragging me closer. I tangled my hands in his hair earning a deep groan. I could feel how much he wanted me and I wanted nothing more than to give myself to him.

I pulled away, "Maybe... we shouldn't do this here." I gasped. He chuckled breathlessly, pressing his lips to mine again. He pressed my hand to the stone around his neck.

"Okay, but remember, Kalli... this, my life force... is yours when you want it." He said. I grinned at him.

"Let's talk about this more, when you aren't recovering from almost dying." I said and I kissed him again.

The Roots of the Apocalypse
Part 1: Becoming Rose
Melinda Reynolds

"So, do you really want to go? You look a little nervous."

"I would like to. It's been so long since I have seen everyone. This pandemic has had us all locked up for fear of contamination. I know some people venture out for essentials, but I have never been one of them. I always had my things delivered and carried out my job remotely. I've spent so long inside, paranoid about who or what might infect me, I nearly had a nervous breakdown the first time I had to go pickup a package from the post office."

"I remember that." Jake said. "I was walking the dog when I stumbled across a young girl on her hands and knees, crying uncontrollably on the sidewalk. To be honest, I almost left you there. After all, it only takes one touch and then you're Balsa."

"So, why did you help me? I don't think I ever asked. You know, it's funny. I spent eight months alone in my house, refusing human contact, despite when they said it was mostly safe to come outside. I just knew there was some Rot somewhere they missed, or that an infected would just be more clever about hiding, given what they do to purify the ones caught. I protected myself to the best of my ability for a walk ten blocks away and was overwhelmed by block one. My fear of being infected toppled me like an iron weight around my neck. I literally thought my life was over and I hadn't even seen anyone yet. When you and Gandalf came along, I think I had accepted my fate. I was waiting for you to let out that awful scream they talk about. Instead, I was smothered in Gandalf kisses." Rose said.

"Yeah, he knocked you on your butt. Honestly, it's Gandalf you have to thank for my help. When I saw that getup…..covered in goggles, an apron, a friggin' ski suit and those ridiculous flowered dishwashing gloves that went up past your elbows, you reminded me of my Marie when she tries to dress herself. And, had I not helped you up, I'm not sure you would have been able to get past Gandalf on your own. He can be rather persistent. Once you were up though, you had this look in your eyes like someone had just saved you from drowning. I'm not sure I've really recovered from that hug you laid on me." Jake rubbed his neck for effect.

Rose blushed, still embarrassed by her emotional state that day. *It's funny how some people come into your life,* Rose thought.

"Yeah, I guess in all the time I spent avoiding people, what I really missed was people. I missed the barbeques and office banter, I missed giving gifts at Christmas and going to the zoo with friends. Hell, I even missed the smell of too many people crowded together in an elevator. This pandemic upended all of our lives. All the things we took for granted, like going to the gas station or grocery store, were nearly lost to us. To me for sure. I'm not sure how many people I lost or how many I have left. It was so hard to know who to trust that I just didn't trust anyone. I hadn't talked to a single soul in the flesh until the day we met. I was so overcome, I couldn't help myself. When you returned my hug, that terrible weight was gone and I felt whole again. I remembered the smiles of those people taken, my mom included. I remembered why I was alone in my house and how much I didn't want to be. Mostly, I remembered how much I wanted my life back."

Jake watched Rose's face highlighted by the streetlights. A mix of determination and fear played over her features. Her body was tense as she stared at the lit up building across the parking lot.

"Well, I'm glad I bumped into you that day. And, look how far you've come in such a short amount of time. Like I said, we don't have to go in. The fact you made it here is a pretty big deal."

"Nah. I appreciate that, and I love that you're my wingman tonight. If I ever want my life back, I'm gonna have to grab it."

Jake grabbed Rose's hand and gave it a squeeze. "Well, let's go then."

***

Rose scanned the gymnasium for a familiar face. All the guests were maintaining social distancing, which made it somewhat easier to see who was in attendance.

"Oh my gosh! Kathryn! Jake, it's my friend Kathryn from H.R. She worked the floor below mine. We always rode the elevator together and would get Starbucks in the lobby on Fridays. It was silly and we would mostly talk about nothing, but wow...I just can't believe she is here. Can we go talk to her?"

"Hey, this is your party. I'm just along for the ride."

Rose and Jake weaved through the crowd, making

sure to stay on the decorative tiles, laid approximately six feet apart from one another. When Rose reached the tile nearest her friend, she waited patiently for Kathryn to finish her conversation. It did not take long for Kathryn to look in Rose's direction.

"Rose!"

Rose smiled brightly and offered Kathryn a wave. "Yeah. How are you? I can't believe you're here!"

"I know! Same goes for you. It's been so long. If I could, I would so hug you right now!"

"Well, we can give air hugs. Besides, I hear if anyone is caught making physical contact, they are kicked out immediately and reported to authorities. So, we are probably better off not hugging."

They both laughed a half-hearted laugh. This was just another sobering reminder of their new reality. Rose didn't know if things could ever go back to the way they used to be.

"So," Kathryn offered, "did you come with anyone? How have you been? Are you working? I don't think I've seen you in a year or so."

"Yeah, I think our last Starbucks sesh was a couple of weeks before they announced the first Rot. When was that? August? It feels like forever ago. But, I am working from home and have been living like a hermit until recently. Speaking of, I want you to meet my friend Jake."

Rose motioned to Jake, who in turn raised his hand in greeting. Kathryn waved at Jake then said to Rose, "You got yourself the strong, silent type huh? A lot HAS changed!"

Kathryn was making Rose giggle with the ridiculous faces she was making. It was just like old times.

"No, it's nothing like that. Jake is just my friend.

His wife had to stay at home with the kids and she was kind enough to let me borrow him."

"Yeah," Jake said, "and she likes me ALMOST as much as she likes her books, so make sure to get me back in one piece."

They all laughed. To Kathryn, Jake said, "Would you like to take my tile? It would make it easier to talk to Rose. I'm gonna go hold up the wall for a little bit."

"Sure. Thank you."

Kathryn took Jake's place. Rose watched Jake find a path through the people and take a seat on the bleachers.

"Well, you watch him like you're with him. You sure nothing is going on? No summertime lovin'?"

"No Kat!" Rose laughed.

Kathryn raised her hands. "Okay, I'm just making sure. You've never needed a male escort before."

"Honestly, if it weren't for Jake, I wouldn't be here tonight. I'm not sure where I'd be. He and his family have been pretty great in getting me out of my house. I was working on becoming a living legend. Like, I stay in my house for so long that people forget someone actually lives there. Then, in five or six years, kids would walk by and point and talk about how my house is haunted and how at night you can see the lights come on sometimes as they try to catch a glimpse of the ghost lady."

"Were you still gonna pay for your yard to get mowed, or were you going all in?"

"No, definitely keeping the yard mowed. I hate it when the grass gets too high. But, maybe I can put some cobwebs up and play spooky Halloween sounds? Think that would be enough?"

"I think your legend is gonna need some work."

They both laughed and Rose said, "So, what about you? How are you holding up?"

"Things aren't too bad. I got promoted."

"Oh really? That's great! So, what kind of promotion? Are you Lord of the Cubicles now?"

"Better. I'm Queen of the whole damn scene. I'm over all of H.R. now."

"You got Bob's old job?" Rose asked.

"Yep." Kathryn beamed.

"So, what's Bob doing now? Did he retire?"

"Bob's Balsa." Kathryn shrugged. "Or, he was for about twenty minutes, until they purified him. They left him in the North parking lot. He was still smoking and twitching when I clocked back in from lunch."

"God, that's awful. It makes me sick to even think about. Bob was always so sweet." Rose said.

"Yeah, when he was human, he was the one we all admired. Hell, I even drunk kissed him at a Christmas party one year."

Kathryn gave a short laugh. She crossed her arms over her chest and she looked fully at Rose. Kathryn wore a stiff smile and her eyes radiated hate. The next words were nearly growled at Rose.

"I can still taste that Maker's Mark whiskey. Some nights, I have nightmares of Bob. Not about his fat sizzling over the splinters of his wooden bones in the parking lot. No, I have nightmares about that kiss.

It's always the same. We are happy, I lean over to kiss him and when I pull back, Bob is Balsa. He lets out the wood wail and I start to turn. When I wake up, I'm always terrified I have turned in my sleep. That's usually how I start my day...crying and trying to remind myself Bob didn't get me. He was trying though.

The Rot had got into Bob's brain. I was in the office working when someone spotted him through the window. Even on the fourth floor, we could see a wood grain to his skin. It was sick and creepy.

Bob was coming for me because I took his job. We had purifiers posted around the building though, and two of them took him down. He was smiling with his wooden arm outstretched towards the purifiers when they lit him up. SMILING! It still gives me the creeps." Kathryn visibly shook.

"Wow, I didn't know. But, why did you think Bob was coming for you? How would he even know you had his job?"

Kathryn made a supreme look of disgust and said, "How should I know? Maybe he kept in touch with people from the office. The point is, I don't think it's some coincidence Bob showed up here after he turned and I just so happened to have his job!"

Rose put her hands up. "Hey Kat, it's okay. I'm just trying to wrap my head around it is all. As for Bob showing up here, I hear people who change retain at least some memory. Many of them go to what is most familiar to that person. That's what makes the contamination so dangerous. How long did Bob work here? Like twenty years or so?"

Kathryn looked at Rose through narrowed eyes. "Are you a tree hugger Rose? An oh no O-chro? A pyra pirate?"

All of these were derogatory slurs for people who sympathized with the contaminated.

"In fact," Kathryn continued, "who is Jake? Maybe he turned you and both came here to turn all of us. I hear the longer you are Balsa, the more human you can appear."

Rose was starting to panic in earnest, but for a different reason.

"Kathryn, that's silly. Come talk to Jake with me. You will see that's not true."

"No, I don't think I will."

"I will just go get him. Be right back."

Rose forced a smile she hoped looked genuine enough. She turned and started walking towards the bleachers, mentally trying to recount how many purifiers were stationed around the building. They were not the type to ask questions before they leveled a flamethrower at you.

Jake looked up as Rose plastered on a fake smile, but her voice was panicked.

"We need to go. Now! Do you have your keys?"

Jake peered around Rose without moving his head. He plastered on an equally fake smile and even managed to look like he was laughing.

"Does it have anything to do with why Kathryn is on her phone right now?"

"She is?" Rose turned to look at Kathryn. Rose smiled and gave her the "one minute" gesture. Kathryn spoke something into her phone without responding to Rose.

When Rose turned her attention back to Jake, he said "Okay, here's how this is gonna go. I'm going to stand up and then we are going to run like our lives depend on it, because they will. Understand?"

Rose nodded. Jake maintained his false smile. If anyone was watching, besides Kathryn, it would look like two people having a polite conversation. Jake stood up and they both ran like Hell. Rose could have sworn she heard a shrill voice saying "Tree huggers" over the faint music and the swell of conversations. She couldn't be sure. Once they left the gym, there was only her adrenaline-fueled heartbeat in her ears. Rose kept repeating "two right and a left" to herself like a mantra. It was just a few hallways and part of a parking lot to freedom.

They were one hallway away from the exit when

a purifier rounded the corner. He certainly looked the part, dressed in an all white hazmat suit, white boots and a flamethrower. A regular angel of death sent to rid this world of potential contaminates and their sympathizers.

Jake and Rose passed him in a dead run. Rose did not waste time to scream or energy in looking back. She did not bother worrying if the heat she felt licking up her spine was from the adrenaline in her muscles or from a purifier's flame. She just kept her eyes on Jake and ran. Jake blew through the exit and Rose was just a few feet behind him. She did not know if he noticed the second purifier coming at them from the corner of the building. Probably not.

Rose caught a metallic glint in Jake's hand. Smart man that he was, he already had his keys in his hand. The purifiers were at least one hundred feet behind them. The flamethrowers used by the purifiers could only shoot up to thirty feet. It gave Rose and Jake a small margin of error.

Jake reached the car a few seconds before Rose. He had the doors open and was behind the wheel when Rose jumped in her seat screaming "Go!", as if that was not the plan. Jake peeled out as the flames from the first flamethrower reached his back windshield. Five minutes after the getaway, Jake was the first to speak.

"So, we are gonna take the long way home. I have another place right outside of town. We are gonna stop there first. What you say between here and there will determine what we do after."

"Should I be worried? What's this stop we're gonna make? Are you gonna turn me in?"

Jake looked at Rose confused and said, "Why would I turn you in? You're not wood grained."

"I know, but that didn't stop Kathryn."

"Look, I don't know your friend….." Jake started.

"I think it's safe to say Kathryn is no longer my friend."

"Okay, I don't know your ex-friend very well but, as an ex-purifier, I do know people. Put enough fear into them and they would turn over their own parents to the flame. I have seen it happen. And, a blanket of fear has covered this nation since news of the first Rot got out. Kathryn has let fear contaminate her, and it's made her dangerous. I'm not afraid of you and you're not infected, okay?"

"Okay, but you were a purifier? I didn't think you could just quit once you signed up."

"You can't, but I did. That was several states ago, not too long after all of this started. What can I say? A year's salary up front, then weekly hazard pay? It sounded too good to be true. I had lost my job, I had kids to feed, So I signed up. You know they give that year's salary in advance because the flamethrowers have a tendency to explode thirty percent of the time? That's not something they tell the public. I'm not innocent in all of this Rose. I've burned Balsa. It was my job. I never enjoyed it like some of these guys, but I did it." Jake waited for Rose's reaction.

"I'm so sorry Jake." Rose said.

Jake shook his head and continued. "I don't know how you don't hate me after hearing something like that. I hate me. I hate me every day since I left. My tipping point was the nursing home. Before that, our unit was just catching random Balsa here or there, but mostly we were burning down areas thought to be contaminated with Rot."

Jake took his eyes from the road to glance at Rose. She was turned towards him in her seat, her face blank save for a small frown. With his eyes back on the road, Jake said "So, a day comes we get distress called to a nursing home. One of the workers was contaminated and came through the back door, just as he always had before. He had touched at least five people that they knew of. By the time we got there, quite a few of the staff and some of the residents were waiting outside. They looked relieved to see us, like we had come to save them. I thought we had. Some of them were pointing at the building, trying to give us details.

Captain got on his radio, then called out a 'Red12'. It was code for 'burn it all', people included. The crowd outside baked first. I was paralyzed by what I was seeing. Everything around me just slowed down, you know? When the people inside started screaming, I just ran."

"Oh my God Jake!"

"Yeah." Jake said, almost a whisper. After a moment of silence, Jake cleared his throat to continue. "In theory, I knew a scenario like that was always a possibility. Turns out, I don't have the heart for that kind of work. Burning the infected was bad enough, but those people outside hadn't changed. You gotta be Balsa for at least a week before you can start to hide your grain. They weren't infected and they still burned."

Rose watched a few tears silently fall from Jake's face. He made no effort to wipe them away.

"At first, I ran like my body was on autopilot. Their screams were in my head, driving my legs. To this day, I don't remember when I went from running to walking. At some point, I just was. I walked and stayed out of sight, until I found a car I could use. It was only when I bent down over a dead man, rummaging through his pockets for his keys, that I noticed I had pissed myself. Thinking back on it now, I must have been in shock. At one point when I was walking, I saw this beautiful, green girl dressed like some warrior princess.

She was chopping the arms off a contaminated corpse. I'm guessing it wasn't the purifiers that killed that one. So yeah, I was a little out of my head."

"Green Xena? Let's hope that was shock." Rose laughed. "So, how did you end up here?"

"Well, I called Beth, told her we were running and to be ready. I chunked the phone, picked up the family and we drove to a place that had no ties to either of us. That's it, in a nutshell. The quarantine has kind of worked to our advantage."

"Wow, I never knew."

"Well, it's not something I can just tell people." Jake smiled at Rose and said, "You gonna turn me in?"

Rose laughed and appeared relieved. "No, I think it's best I stay away from the authorities for now. You're good. So, what did you need to know anyhow? You said earlier it would determine what we do next?"

"Basically, I just need to know if you had put my name down on anything having to do with that reunion? Have you ever talked about my family on social media? Does anyone there know where you live or know your family? Do you have a phone on you? Is there any way anyone can track you?"

"I don't do phones. I'm probably the only person alive with a landline. I use my computer at home for work and social media. I'm not really active on my media accounts anymore and I have never mentioned you guys to anyone. Not that I don't love you all, I just don't talk to anyone but you. My address is registered with work, and Kat for sure knows where I live. The only family I have is my mom, and she's gone now."

"So, other than seeing me at the reunion, they can't find me?"

"Yeah, that's about right."

"Well, you for sure can't go back home. Maybe

you can prove you're not infected, but I don't see that happening. So, new plan. I'm gonna drop you off and you can get cleaned up. Use some of Beth's clothes to change into. Do not make any calls and do not leave, okay?"

"All right. What about you?"

"After I drop you off, I will grab the family and all of us will come back. We will stay for a week or so and make sure no one shows up at our place looking for me. It will give us some time to figure out what to do next."

"I don't know what to say. Thank you."

Jake pulled the car down a dark, gravel road. "You don't have to say anything. We are friends, and we just so happen to both be fugitives. What are the odds?" Jake smiled, but Rose could tell he was exhausted. Jake turned beside a mailbox before the road terminated.

"C'mon," Jake said, "let's get you inside."

Jake led Rose to the door of a quaint, country home. There was a menacing quality to the darkened doorstep. Rose felt like she was being watched. She felt like her life was in a spiral and she would cease to be the minute she walked into Jake's house. *But, that's just it. Life as I know it is over,* Rose thought.

***

Rose had showered and changed, just as Jake suggested. She paced the house and more than a few times was drawn to the windows, checking to make sure neither the authorities or any "Balsa Bobs" were coming for her. She resigned herself to looking at the family photos in the hall and the food in the kitchen cabinet. She was too on edge to sit. She was making a glass of tea when she heard a vehicle pull up. She left the steaming cup on the counter and ran to the guest room. She figured if it was the authorities, they would bust in the doors, so she would go out the window. Not a great plan, but better than nothing. *I guess I will need a new plan if they torch the house,* Rose thought.

Rose heard the front door open, followed by the sound of giggles and little feet running upstairs.

"Rose?" Jake called out.

Rose went back to the kitchen to find Beth putting away food and Jake setting down bags.

"Hey guys."

"Oh, hey." Jake said. "I see you found everything."

"Yes, thank you. How was the trip?"

"I'm assuming you don't mean the scenery." Jake said. "We weren't followed, we have enough stuff here to last a few months and the kids are happy to get out of the house. Also, we made the news."

"What?!"

"Yeah, we are being reported as 'potential contaminates'. They are using your employee picture and a grainy pic of us walking into the building."

"I'm so sorry I got you guys into this."

"Hey," Jake motioned to himself, "fugitive already, remember? You didn't do anything you have to apologize for."

"No, but if I'm caught they will still burn me and all of you too. This is insane! I just had a conversation and now my life is over!"

Jake walked to Rose and put his hands on her shoulders causing a dam to break. She was pale, wide-eyed and sobbing. "Hey now, we aren't dead yet, okay? In fact, new rule. No dying. It's been a long day. Let me show you to your room so I can help Beth with the kids. We all need some sleep."

Rose let Jake lead her to the guest room. He pulled back the covers on the bed, and she didn't wait for the invitation. She was asleep as soon as her head hit the pillow.

***

Rose awoke the next day from a dreamless sleep. Life was already full swing around the house and it brought a great deal of normalcy Rose desperately needed. For a few days, that's what she got. The kids played, the adults cooked and cleaned, and everyone came together for meals while Gandalf foraged for scraps at their feet. After the kids went to bed, the adults would settle down for a movie and wine. Rose never shook the feeling of being watched.

***

Day four started like all the rest. Jake confirmed they were still wanted. Purifiers had burned Rose's house down. The kids played with Gandalf. Food was on the stove and Beth was looking for something.

"Hey Rose?" Beth said.

"Yeah, what's up?"

"I need to run up to the barn. I think the hose attachment I'm looking for is up there. Gandalf needs a bath. He's starting to smell like dog. Can you keep an eye on stuff for me?"

"Yeah, nada problem."

Rose watched Beth making her way to the barn at the back of the property. She walked down a well worn path through the tall grass. The path curved out of sight about one hundred feet in and swallowed Beth up.

Rose's hands were suddenly clammy and there was a low level buzz in her head. Rose did not just *feel* like someone was watching her, she *knew* it. Rose went to the foot of the stairs and yelled up to Jake.

Jake popped his head over the top of the banister and said, "Yeah, what's up?"

"Hey, Beth ran up to the barn by herself. I can't see her anymore and I think maybe we aren't alone."

"What?! Did you see someone?"

"No, but I have been feeling like we're being watched since we got here. Are you able to see the barn from upstairs?"

"One sec." Jake disappeared. Rose heard him going in and out of the rooms.

Jake popped his head back over the rail and said, "Beth was almost to the barn and I think she might have been skipping. If there's anyone out there, they're ninjas. I checked all the windows just to be safe. There's no one, Rose.

Also, I may have decommissioned several of Braxton's army men in my rush to get to their window. Brax was not amused. I told him the army dudes couldn't hope to win against Marie's army of Glitter Ponies. Gandalf chuffed and licked Brax's face like he agreed! Can you believe it?"

"He is pretty smart." Rose agreed. "So, Beth is okay?"

"Yeah, and I imagine she will be back anytime. Did she say what she went up there for?"

"Some attachment to wash Gandalf with?"

"Well then, I know she won't be long. She probably forgot the last time we were out here she organized the barn. Is the food almost done?"

"Yeah." Rose said.

"Then, let me come down and give you a hand."

***

Rose and Jake made a good team. Rose made the plates and Jake set the table. Rose's head wasn't buzzing anymore and she decided it was probably just anxiety. Rose had finished making the last plate when Beth walked back in.

"Hey hun, I was just about to call for the kids." Jake said. He took the finished plate to the table.

Rose noticed Beth standing unnaturally still.

"Beth?" Rose asked.

Beth twitched and she jerked her head to the side to look at Rose.

What's wrong with her face? Is that grain? Rose thought

Rose smiled at Beth. Beth's mouth was slightly open and there was an incandescence to her skin. Beth started to raise her arm and appeared to have trouble doing so.

Jake had his back to the pair. Rose slowly walked backwards to him, never taking her eyes from Beth.

Rose whispered, "Hey Jake? You need to get the kids and the dog and we need to go. Beth is infected."

Jake stopped what he was doing, sighed and said, "Look Rose, I know you're having a lot of anxiety right now and that's completely understandable. But, you gotta keep it together. How would she even get infected? No one's here but us."

"Maybe someone's hiding in the barn."

"Well, no one was there when I stashed the car."

"Beth isn't acting right, Jake."

"Okay, I will check on Beth. Why don't you go get the kids for me?"

Beth remained where she was, but Rose did not see any twitching or unnatural glowing skin.

Rose walked away and shook her head. *Maybe I am losing it.*

Jake turned to see Rose walking towards the stairs and Beth quickly walking after her. Beth's arm was outstretched and her jaw was unhinged to her chest. Beth was wood grained.

"Rose, run!" Jake yelled as he ran to intercept his wife.

Jake jumped between the two women, but it was

too late. Beth slammed into the front of her husband and touched Rose over his shoulder.

As Rose stared into the gaping maw of her friend, time slowed down. Her head was buzzing again and she could hear an unfamiliar voice whispering, "She is becoming Rose." Then, the world went dark.

***

Rose awoke in a heap on the floor of an empty warehouse. As she went to push herself off the floor, her hand clacked on the concrete. She scrambled to her feet and touched her face. There was another hollow clack.

Rose slowly lowered her hand. She was not just wood grained, she was solid wood! Rose let out a scream and abruptly covered her mouth, hand clacking against her lips. She ran to the nearest window to see if anyone heard her.

Looking through a dirty window, Rose saw an unfamiliar landscape full of wooden people. Every one of them looked like human-sized puppets, with limbs and joints perfectly crafted. There were small houses and a few buildings, almost all of it overrun by nature.

I'm dreaming. I have to be dreaming!

Rose was so transfixed by the landscape, she didn't hear the door to her left open until a man yelled, "We got a live one."

"Who are you? Stay away from me!"

"Hey now…." The wooden man said, "I'm Collin and you used to be human, right? Me too. No one will hurt you here. Well, no one wooden anyway. I'm here to help."

Rose eyed him suspiciously.

"Have you seen yourself yet?" Collin asked.

"I've seen enough to know I'm not human. Oh God!" Rose wailed. "Saying it out loud REALLY puts it into a new perspective, doesn't it?"

"Ummmm, yeah. There's something else you should probably see before we go any further. But, just know this is normal for the people here." Collin handed Rose a mirror.

Rose took the mirror. Her hand clacked on her cheek as she touched Beth's face.

So, my mind is in Beth's wooden body like some kind of Freakier Friday?

"I think you need to tell me what's going on, Collin."

To be continued…...

About the Authors

Anchorette Roussseau

Anchorette Rousseau is a writer of all things erotic horror, bringing the fears from deep in our psyches to the surface and shining a light on them for all to see.

C.J. Wood

C.J. Wood is a whiskey drinking, wine loving, book hoarder. She spends her days reading, writing, and hanging out with her pets on her ever growing farm.

Carrie Humphrey

Living in a small town in North Carolina, Carrie enjoys writing, reading, traveling, and hanging out with her three kids, husband, spoiled dog, and cranky cat. Her series, The Briarberry Estate, is internationally read, and when she's not submerged in the paranormal world, she enjoys writing romance short stories of every flavor.

K.R. Cervantez

K.R Cervantez is happily married with an amazing family. She is also wonderfully nerdy in all the best ways. When not writing, she is enjoying a good book or watching her favorite shows. She likes video games, anime and comic books.

Melinda Reynolds

Melinda is a nurse, mother of three, and is known as the "crazy bunny lady". When she's not spending time with her kids, she is tearing up the town with her husky or hanging with her friends. She loves reading, writing, and the occasional margarita.

Made in the USA
Columbia, SC
24 January 2021

31500299R00057